Ciuleandra

Liviu Rebreanu

Ciuleandra
Liviu Rebreanu

Translation copyright © 2021 Gabi Reigh

FG-RO0001L
ISBN: 978-4-908793-49-3

Copyediting: Marie Deer

Cover © 2021 Daniele Serra

CADMUS PRESS
CADMUSMEDIA.ORG

Ciuleandra

Liviu Rebreanu

Translated by
Gabi Reigh

Introduction by
George T. Sipos

CADMUS PRESS
2021

Contents

Liviu Rebreanu: At the Forefront of the Romanian Modern Novel Tradition

George T. Sipos

LIVIU REBREANU (1885–1944) IS one of the most important literary voices in Romania's interwar period. Hailing from rural Transylvania, Rebreanu was a novelist and prose writer, a playwright and translator, an iconic figure in the world of letters and a member of the golden generation of modernist writers alongside Mihail Sadoveanu (1880–1961), Camil Petrescu (1894–1957), Hortensia Papadat-Bengescu (1876–1955), Mircea Eliade (1907–86), Mateiu I. Caragiale (1885–1936), and Panait Istrati (1884–1935), a generation that shaped the evolution of Romanian literature well into the postwar period and beyond. Rebreanu's early experimentation with various novelistic formats was crucial for the success of contemporary and subsequent writers alike and demonstrated the maturity of the modern Romanian language and national psyche to engage with the ample breadth of the architecture and style of the novel.

Liviu Rebreanu was born in 1885 in the small Transylvanian village of Târlişua, then part of the Austro-Hungarian Empire and today in the county of Bistriţa Năsăud, in Romania. The eldest of fourteen siblings, Liviu was the son of Vasile (1863–1914), a rural elementary school teacher—and as such, a member of the village intelligentsia—and Ludovica (1865–1945), a talented amateur actress, well-known locally.

An ethnic Romanian, Rebreanu was educated in Hungarian and German, first in Transylvania, then in Hungary, and showed an excellent aptitude for the study of foreign languages and humanities. Although attracted by the study of medicine, he enrolled at the Ludoviceum Military Academy in Budapest in 1903. Upon graduation, he was dispatched as a young sublieutenant of the Austro-Hungarian military to Gyula, in Hungary. That is where he began to write seriously short stories and plays, all in Hungarian.

His debut in Romanian took place after his resignation from the military, in 1908, with the novella *Codrea (Glasul inimii)* (Codrea, The Voice of the Heart), published in the literary magazine *Luceafărul* from Sibiu. In 1909, by now an aspiring writer and well-known journalist, Rebreanu crossed the Carpathians into Romania and moved to Bucharest. At the request of the Austro-Hungarian authorities, however, he was arrested in 1910 and extradited back to Gyula where he served a short prison term on a charge of journalism activities contravening national interests. One of his major early novellas, *Golanii* (The Thugs, 1916) was completed in prison, as were a number of translations from the works of his good friend, Hungarian writer Szini Gyula (1876–1932), which would be published a few years later in Romanian literary magazines. Most of these writings are gathered in the prose volume *Frământări* (Anxieties, 1912), published by a small regional press.

The following years were full of troubles and financial concerns. Rebreanu tried various journalist positions and worked for theaters and literary magazines, always in pursuit of stable employment, always hoping for a breakthrough in the literary world. In 1912, he married

Ștefana Rădulescu, an actress from the National Theater of Craiova in southern Romania, where he was working as the literary secretary. The couple moved to Bucharest that same year, and Rebreanu was finally accepted as a member of the Romanian Writers' Society. While his wife found work immediately at the National Theater of Bucharest, Liviu was only able to become a reporter for the major daily, *Adevărul*, where he was retained only until Romania's victory in the Second Balkan War of 1912–13.

World War I brought more hardship to the Rebreanus. In December 1916, German troops occupied Bucharest, and the writer—as a former officer in the Austro-Hungarian army—found himself in danger of facing arrest again. He began to work frantically on his first novelistic masterpiece, the rural fresco novel, *Ion* (1920). He was arrested in 1918 but managed to escape and flee to the eastern province of Moldavia, where the Romanian government had found refuge and was organizing a counter-offensive against the occupation armies. Sadly, Rebreanu's family had been hit with another personal tragedy the year before, when the writer's younger brother, Emil, an officer himself in the Austro-Hungarian army and an ethnic Romanian, was accused of attempted desertion and espionage on behalf of the Romanians and executed. Emil's fate and the tragedy of Romanian soldiers forced to fight a war against their own people found literary illustration in the 1922 novel *Pădurea spânzuraților* (The Forest of the Hanged).

With *Ion* and *The Forest of the Hanged*, Rebreanu entered a new stage in his creative maturity, his literary prowess now recognized at the national level. Moreover, the writer realized the need for a variety of narrative voices and experimentation with various writing methods. From 1920 to the end of his literary career, Rebreanu published nine novels, all different in theme and narrative approach. *Ion* and *The Forest of the Hanged* were followed by *Adam și Eva* (Adam and Eve, 1925), *Ciuleandra* (Ciuleandra, 1927), *Crăișorul* (The Prince, 1929), *Răscoala* (The Uprising, 1932), *Jar* (Ambers, 1934), *Gorila* (The Gorilla, 1938), and *Amândoi* (Both, 1940).

These novels brought his name and artistry to the public's attention, and some, such as *The Forest of the Hanged*, brought him national awards and medals. A public figure now, Rebreanu was appointed the Director of the National Theater of Bucharest, and served in governmental positions, such as manager of the People's Education Secretariat in the Ministry of Education. Widely received and enjoyed by the readership of the time, Rebreanu's novels were reviewed and discussed in literary and cultural magazines, with *Ciuleandra*—rendered in English in this volume—becoming the first book made into a movie with sound in Romanian, in 1930. Nominated by his fellow novelist, Mihail Sadoveanu, Rebreanu was elected in 1939 a member of the prestigious Romanian Academy.

Rebreanu had a final opportunity to represent Romanian culture worldwide through a series of lectures throughout Germany and the annexed Austria, Zagreb and Weimar in 1942, the last two trips on behalf of the Pan-European Culture Society. He then withdrew from public life, his health deteriorating. In April 1944, he left Bucharest for his countryside residence, never to return. His ravaged lungs gave out on September 1, 1944, in Valea Mare, in Argeș County, not far from where part of the plot in *Ciuleandra* unfolds and where he wrote his major 1932 work, *The Uprising*. Although initially buried there, his body was moved to Bucharest only a few months later and his remains interred in the Bellu Cemetery, where most major modern Romanian writers and artists rest.

Liviu Rebreanu's literary work spans more than three decades and is usually associated with the Romanian literary inclination to focus on the life of the peasants, on the rural, and on the agrarian. No surprise there, of course, given the traditional occupations of the inhabitants of the lands north of the Danube River and nestled within the arch of the Carpathians. For millennia, Romanians, and the Dacians before them, have been farmers and shepherds. Raised in Transylvanian villages at the beginning of the twentieth century, it is no wonder that Rebreanu's first inspiration and the strongest, most consistent thread of his literary work lies there, in the heart of a peasant geographical and human landscape. But, in the good spirit of the *Narodnik* literature of Russia's second half of the nineteenth century, that same vein of literary inspiration that guided the works of Maksim Gorky and which in Romania materialized in the early-twentieth-century literary current of *Sămănătorism* (Sower-ism), Rebreanu was generally attracted by the people of the margins: the poor, the illiterate, the forgotten. They are famished and angry tenant farmers, members of the *lumpenproletariat*, violent suburban dwellers, village priests and dirty pub owners, lowly soldiers, all caught in the claws of modern life, subjugated by higher-ranking officers, tricked by those with more money and knowledge of life than themselves. As a result, they focus on almost grotesque amorous obsessions, are ready to jump into fistfights, beat their wives or mistresses, and even commit rape and otherwise let themselves be overwhelmed by raging violence.

When analyzing those early novellas and stories populated by characters very much aligned with and inspired by the rural world where the writer spent his childhood, literary critic G. Călinescu would rightfully note: "Focusing on servants, valets, petty thieves and petty bourgeois types, he (Rebreanu) focuses in fact on the obscure psychology of human beings dehumanized by poverty and longing, those who painstakingly save their meager income, and then burst out suddenly, disproportionately, in curses and fistfights."[1] These are indeed, as Călinescu added, the first of Rebreanu's attempts at "psychological investigation" into the "dark, quasi-animalistic soul, one processing slowly and with much difficulty and exploding fiercely, with extraordinary violence."[2]

Rebreanu's later and more voluminous works, the nine novels, are usually classified into three different categories, based on their overarching themes. Four, *Ion, The Prince, The Uprising,* and *The Gorilla,* are focused on social issues; four, *The Forest of the Hanged, Adam and Eve, Ciuleandra,* and *Ambers,* on psychological trauma and the way individual characters deal with it, and one, *Both,* is a murder mystery.

Generally speaking, however, Rebreanu's name and contribution to modern Romanian literature remains overwhelmingly associated with *Ion* and *The Uprising* as frescoes of the Romanian village at the beginning of the twentieth century, and with *The Forest of the Hanged,* as a psychological novel. The first, set in the village of Prislop, in Transylvania, is populated with several of the characters Rebreanu had developed previously in his short stories and novellas. The story focuses on the evolution of a peasant, Ion Pop al Glanetaşului, who will stop at nothing to gain the only fortune he can imagine, land. Cunning and relentless, he has been interpreted by Romanian literary critics either as the perfect parvenu, in the vein of Balzac's nineteenth century series of Realist novels and novellas *La comédie humaine* (The Hu-

---

1   G. Călinescu (1982). *Istoria literaturii române de la origini până în prezent.* București: Minerva, 731.
2   Idem.

man Comedy), such as E. Lovinescu,[3] or as a "brute, for whom cunning replaces intelligence," such as G. Călinescu.[4] More sympathetic critics of the postwar period, such as Al. Piru did feel the need to retort to this rather dismissive description of the character. In his 1965 work on Liviu Rebreanu, Al. Piru wrote: "Lovinescu's characterization can lead to the wrong conclusion that Ion is nothing but a lifeless abstraction, the embodiment of a monomania, while that of Călinescu to the paradoxical conclusion that there can't possibly be intelligent humans in the countryside."[5]

Rather than following one individual and his obsessions (the ardent desire to possess, either land or, in the latter half of the novel, a woman), *The Uprising* tends to focus on the rural masses and was inspired by the 1907 violent tenant farmer uprising against poverty, famine, and misery at the hands of absentee landlords, a social movement ended in a bloodbath by the authorities of the time. The background is now eastern and southern Romanian villages, one that is less familiar to the writer. And, perhaps for that reason, he is best when it comes to describing masses. A psychological novel on its own, albeit one focused on the group, we find here one of the best exemplifications of what French psychologist and sociologist Gustave Le Bon (1841–1931) called "psychology of the masses." The novel "marks the highest point in the development of the novelist" and it is where "the singularity of Rebreanu's writings appears plainer within the context of world fiction of the thirties [...]."[6]

Published in 1922, *The Forest of the Hanged* is a war

3 E. Lovinescu (1998). *Istoria literaturii române contemporane.* Chișinău: Litera, 219–20.
4 Idem, 732.
5 Al. Piru (1965). *Liviu Rebreanu.* București: Meridiane, XII.
6 Mircea Zaciu (1986). "Foreword" in Liviu Rebreanu, *Adam and Eve.* Translated from the Romanian by Mihail Bogdan. Bucharest: Minerva Publishing House, X.

novel inspired by the tragedy of Rebreanu's own brother, sublieutenant Emil Rebreanu, who was executed in 1917 for trying to desert and join the Romanian army during World War I. In a world dominated by war, the main character, Apostol Bologa, a young Romanian officer in the Austro-Hungarian army, faces a moral dilemma when he is dispatched to the Romanian front where he must fight against fellow Romanians. Timid and predisposed to philosophical musings, Bologa struggles with the conflict between his duty as an officer and his belonging to the Romanian nation. The novel is equally interesting to critic Ion Bogdan Lefter "through the multiethnic subject matter." Bologa's situation is a "particular case of identity drama undergone then by Czech, German, Jewish and other soldiers alike."[7] An early premonitory scene in the novel depicts the execution of Czech officer Svoboda, in the same way the main character will be dispatched.

Most of Rebreanu's work has been relatively well translated into a variety of languages, with some works, such as *Ciuleandra*, being translated immediately after publication in Romanian, a sign of the worldwide recognition the writer had come to enjoy. In addition to 1930's *Ciuleandra*, most of Rebreanu's other novels have been made into films: *The Uprising* and *The Forest of the Hanged* in 1965, *Ion*, with the title, *Ion, Blestemul pământului, blestemul iubirii* (Ion, The Curse of the Land, The Curse of Love), in 1979, a remake of *Ciuleandra* in 1985, and *Adam and Eve* in 1990, with the first two enjoying excellent public receptions.

The short novel in this volume is singular within Rebreanu's work as it delves deeper than anywhere else

---

7 Ion Bogdan Lefter (1999). *A Guide to Romanian Literature: Novels, Experiment and The Postcommunist Book Industry.* Pitești: Paralela 45, 30.

into the psyche of a character giving voice to his innermost thoughts and feelings. Set in the interwar period, the plot is centered on Puiu Faranga, a descendant of an old *boyar* (Romanian nobility) family. As such, he is the beneficiary of wealth, prestige, and the assurance of a safe and well-rewarded position within the political realm without needing to achieve much on his own. His father, Polycarp, already a prominent politician, is worried about the family genetics, which have been altered, he believes, by centuries of intermarriage. His decision to mitigate the danger he perceives in his only son ultimately leads to the tragic event that opens the story and Puiu's light—a privilege due to his wealth and social status—incarceration in a mental asylum. Rebreanu's intent with the novel was to capture the very essence of madness, by showing the thin line between normality and insanity, and how, in effect, any seemingly sane person can easily slide into insanity.

The pretext for this Dostoevskian adventure is a crime, Puiu's murder of his wife. In his own words, Rebreanu explained his intentions with *Ciuleandra* in his diary entry for August 8, 1927: "*Ciuleandra* is for me a work where I express and clarify a major mystery of the heart, in this case, the so-often invoked love that leads to murder. I tackled it simply, without complication, so it might not please all those who love complicated and twisted plots. But this is how I felt it [...]. At any rate, what do I know? If it so happens that the book won't find any success with the public, so be it. It will always be dear to me because I captured instincts in it."[8]

While the psychological introspection exercise has its own positive aspects in *Ciuleandra*, where Rebreanu re-

---

8 Liviu Rebreanu (1968–98). *Opere, vol. 1–18*. București: Minerva, 17: 7. Vol. 17: *Jurnal (1927–44)*, critical edition by Niculae Gheran.

mains magistral is in the description of groups moving together, animated by unleashed energy, in full contact with the universe and capable of anything while acting together. That is, in fact, the scene of the Ciuleandra dance, an ancient tradition from southern Romania, a new height of Rebreanu's artistic ability to depict mass movements. The Ciuleandra dance is reminiscent of circular pre-Christian sun-worshiping rituals prevalent in all regions of Romania. Ciuleandra is a ritual rehearsal of the life cycle itself. The song starts very slowly, and the tempo increases gradually to end in a frenzy of life-affirming energy. As such, the dance is also a great opportunity for uninitiated youth to grasp the meaning of life, an occasion for young men and women to get together and let themselves become enraptured in an almost orgiastic pre-marital rite, and to prepare them for the fast pace of adult life.

Ciuleandra, the song and the dance, represent the perfect vehicle for the old Faranga *boyar* to find a commoner female partner for his son. Here is a brief fragment of Rebreanu's description of the dance, in Gabi Reigh's excellent translation into English: "The ring of dancers, daring themselves to defy and smother the music's spell, charge at it, feet crushing into dirt, and the tornado of flesh twists into itself again, tighter, more stubborn, tightening and loosening, until, finally, the bodies melt into each other like a fallen harvest. There, fixed in that spot, for a few minutes, for an eternity, possessed by the same maniacal rhythm, the bodies of men and women knead into each other, quivering, thrumming. Once in a while the simmering passion is pierced by long shrieks, erupting as if from ancient depths, or by the startled cry of a girl whose breasts were clenched too tightly… And that's how it would go on until each dancer's soul melted into that all-encompassing flame of unbridled passion."

The ensuing tragedy however is more than anything a symbol of the inability of the noble class to adapt to the new reality that is taking over the world in the guise of modernity. Faranga's attempt to ensure that his bloodline continues comes to an untimely end, and the attempt to maintain the status quo by inducting a peasant woman into the nobility fails miserably. There is no room in the Ciuleandra ritual and its world for those against whom the peasants symbolically direct the violence of their dance moves. Though they may try to invade it (as they do in the novel), the *boyars* will be quickly and unceremoniously expelled. The role played by the young doctor Ursu—whose very last name, meaning "bear", is not only a marker of his peasant origin, but also carries totemic, apotropaic meanings—in Puiu Faranga's ultimate slide into madness is not trifling. It is too late in history for robust peasant blood to save the nobility, which is forever stuck in feudal pretensions and fantasies of superiority. The Farangas, the old *boyars*, like the characters in another Romanian novel from the same period dealing with the decay of Romania's old noble class, Mateiu I. Caragiale's *Craii de Curtea Veche* (Rakes of the Old Court, 1929),[9] are doomed in the face of modern society.

The social and political interpretation above for *Ciuleandra* is a new critical take on the novel. Other critics have said that the novel—locked as it normally was within the framework of a psychological introspection work—was lacking in various ways. Ion Simuț wrote in his foreword to the 2014 edition: "The main flaw of the novel resides in the unbelievable rationality of adopting madness, although it could be said that the author takes that risk and embraces that paradox willingly."[10]

---

9 Mateiu I. Caragiale (2021). *Rakes of the Old Court*. Translated by Sean Cotter. Chicago: Northwestern University Press.
10 Ion Simuț (2014). Foreword. In Liviu Rebreanu, *Ciuleandra*. București: Cartex, VI.

In *Ciuleandra*, we probably see best what Mircea Zaciu once remarked about Rebreanu: "Rebreanu's approach to life and art was the simple straightforward expression of *truth* which, while 'rugged' at times, is the most important thing."[11] Rebreanu was, for all intents and purposes, a modernist writer and a member of the European literary Realist movement in the tradition of Balzac, Flaubert and even Zola. But he was also aligned with the realities of early-twentieth-century Transylvanian emotions and with interwar Romanian society. Rebreanu was an impeccable portraitist who was at his best when it came to groups, and a fine observer of human nature. His main difficulties remained stylistic, evidence of the very incipient nature of the Romanian-language prose and novel construction of his time.

But, as Zaciu said, "Liviu Rebreanu ranks among the outstanding novelists of modern European realism that set forth the problems of the masses; and when he probes into the life of the individual (be that an intellectual, peasant, aristocrat, bourgeois or *lumpen*), he always does it from the standpoint of social destiny, integrated at times into a cosmic horizon. He thus stands as a forerunner of […] modernity…"[12] The roads Liviu Rebreanu opened for Romanian modern prose-writing and novel architecture are still valid and relevant today, almost a century after the production of most of his work.

---

11 Mircea Zaciu. *Idem*, VII.
12 Idem, XI.

Ciuleandra

...and knowest not that thou art wretched, and miserable, and poor, and blind, and naked.

—*Revelations, 3: 17*

I

'QUIET! QUIET! QUIET!'

He had hurled her onto the sofa, his right knee crushing her breasts. His fingers pressed down into her soft, pale throat, trying to smother an answer he dreaded to hear. He could feel her body writhing as if in an ardent embrace, inflaming his fury.

'Quiet! Quiet!'

He chanted the same word, in the same hoarse voice, in between long, painful gulps of air. His swollen eyes grew blind to everything, sinking beneath a red, heavy veil. . . . At last, he felt a faint pressure on his arms, only for a few moments, and then sensed it melting away, defeated. He realised, as though in a dream, that the pressure he had felt must have been her arms, as she tried to defend herself. And then, all of a sudden and very clearly, he heard his own voice, raw, broken, breathless, echoing from the pit of a dungeon. 'What a voice!'—the thought flashed through his mind and then, his vision suddenly returning, he noticed two white globes, glassy, straining out of their sockets, with a fine web of delicate red veins clustered around a violet-blue stain: her eyes, fixed in a gaze of terror and resignation.

Her stare taunted him with its insufferable reproach:

'Qu . . . ie . . .'

He wanted to shout, but now the sound crumbled in his throat, dry, rattling, while the white globes kept on growing and melting together into an ashen shadow that started to whirl around the frozen blue stain, vertiginously. His arms slackened as he began to faint. He caught himself falling and searched, desperate, for something to lean on. . . .

Released from the nightmare, he stumbled three steps backwards. His stiff fingers curled into claws. He looked around, bewildered.

He strained to focus. The rays of the electric lightbulbs, synthetic and yellow, hurt him, as though he were suddenly emerging from complete darkness into blinding light. Everything around him was distorted, unfamiliar. Next to the sofa, the white bearskin rug bristled and the head with its dead glass eyes stared at him, the open mouth menacingly baring its fangs. In the hearth, two logs crackled amidst the golden flames that twisted and stretched wrathfully, like the tongue of a dragon. In between the two windows that looked out onto the street, the dressing table, with its mirror rising to the ceiling, and laden with puffs, jars, bottles and other such objects belonging to the arsenal of feminine beautification, stood like a creature frozen with shame.

He reached the door of the bedroom, smoothing down his crumpled cuffs and sleeves, his dazed eyes drawn again and again to the sofa where her motionless body lay, her head tilted towards him, her bare chest rising from the ruffled dress. Millions of thoughts stormed through his mind, colliding together with a muffled noise. When, eventually, his heart had settled, he observed that the only sound in the room was his own exhausted breath; aside from that, only silence, tender, mollifying; even the fire now burned so quietly it might have been a mere illusion. The heat was suffocating. Sweat poured down his cheeks like tears. And yet the worst was still the silence and so, to chase it away, he called out:

'Madeleine!'

He had tried to sound gentle, yet the menacing, unfamiliar voice frightened him. He recalled how that same voice had surprised him earlier when . . . And all of a sudden he was overwhelmed by a great mortification, as if he had stumbled naked into a jeering crowd. He realised that, although he had fixed his eyes on the sofa, his spirit turned away from the sight, petrified, delaying the moment when he would have to face his deed.

'Madeleine!' he murmured again, humbly, praying that one word could atone for all.

The next few moments flickered past as he weighed every possible truth: that she was alive and that she was dead, that he had murdered her or he had not, that nothing had happened and that everything had ended. . . . Beneath it all, the memory of a thought, when he had hurled himself towards her, ringing in his brain like a decree: that he must kill her and yet she would not die. . . .

All of a sudden, with a shiver of fear, he found himself face to face with a young man with black, slightly dishevelled hair, a clean-shaven, fine-boned, oval, ravaged face, wandering eyes, dressed in a dinner jacket with the cuffs slipping out of the sleeves, the collar rising up stiffly towards one ear, like an aristocrat in an American film after a scuffle with a rival landowner. . . .

He startled, recognising his own face in the mirror.

'Poor Puiu Faranga!' he said, a forlorn smile answering back from the glass.

The grimace instantly froze on his face like a mask. In the mirror, from the sofa, her head slightly tilted to the side, Madeleine watched him with those wide, white eyes and a mocking expression.

Confounded, he staggered towards her, but a noise cut him short. Madeleine's arm, rounded and white, slipped to the floor, skimming the neck of the bear as though caressing it.

Now the truth unveiled itself in a flash to Puiu Fa-ranga.

Her eyes seemed alive, her arm arranged itself into a living gesture—and it was exactly all this that proclaimed to him clearly that there was no hope. The terror that he had extinguished a human life twisted in his soul like a dagger. He didn't know what to do, and this helplessness filled him with horror as he drowned in that stifling silence.

He turned his back to her with grim determination, as if tearing his feet out of a clamp, and made for the door of the bedroom, wanting to leave. Through the root of his spine, he felt a hand pursuing him, dragging him back. . . .

II

He was walking falteringly, unsteadily, like a drunk. He passed through another bedroom where a single blue lightbulb glowed like a watchful eye, then through a dark sitting room, finally emerging into the hall where the crude bright lights assaulted his senses as he rushed towards a closed door; there, he stopped, all his strength drained away. He somehow found himself on the other side, as if blown through the door by a storm, stammering:

'Father! Father!'

Old Policarp Faranga stood up from his desk, alarmed.

Seeing his son, he chided him, anxiously. '*Tu es fou?* Are you mad, my son?'

The sound of his father's voice crushed him. His horror had evaporated and a dizzying despair took its place. He drew near to the desk and collapsed, exhausted, into the large leather armchair.

Still standing, the old man examined his son haughtily, still offended by the discourteous manner he had thrown himself into the armchair without being invited in. The old man was also wearing a dinner jacket and his majestic silver beard, always impeccably groomed, nestled on a chest crammed with military decorations.

He needed to appear stately and presentable at all times, not only in society but even in his private moments. Tall and robust, he wore his sixty-three years with an almost defiant dignity, inspiring spontaneous respect from everyone around him. . . . Faced with Puiu's dejection, he forced himself to break the silence.

'*Mais parle donc, voyons, parle! Qu'est-ce que tu as?* Speak up! What is wrong with you?'

The young man turned his dead, empty eyes towards his father. He wondered how to tell him and fumbled for the right words. He exploded, incoherently:

'Father . . . I . . . I don't know . . . Madeleine is dead. . . .'

Faranga shuddered, the words splitting his heart open like an arrow:

'What are you saying. . . ? Madeleine? You. . . ? Impossible!'

He tried to read the truth in his son's eyes, but Puiu lowered his head again. The old man fell silent for a while as question after question raced through his mind, leaning on the desk with both hands, rooted to the spot like an unseasoned judge in front of an inscrutable defendant. At last, he walked to the other side of the desk where Puiu sat and put his hand on his son's shoulder.

'Where is. . . ?'

He didn't finish the question, nor did he wait for the answer for more than a second. His movement away from his desk had suddenly awakened him and shifted the train of his thoughts, so that he hurried out of the room, leaving the door wide open behind him. . . .

Puiu had sunk into a clouded apathy, motionless, as if he couldn't remember what he was doing there. His thoughts were tangled into an oppressive chaos where nothing that made sense could take shape. Beneath the clutter in his mind, however, his soul grasped clearly the fact that his father had gone to that room to see the proof and be certain that Madeleine had in fact . . .

He could hear distinctly the heavy, urgent steps of the old man and felt the draught entering through the open door. And later Aunt Matilda's voice, breathless and rushed as she ran up the stairs, apologising for being late, but it had not been her fault, only the chauffeur found something wrong with the car just as they were about to leave and he had to repair it. . . .

The answer rose immediately into Puiu's heart: yes, she alone was to blame, for had she not been late, nothing would have happened. . . .

The old man said something to Matilda. Puiu did not catch the words, but as soon as they were spoken he heard Aunt Matilda whimpering and firing questions at old Faranga as she ran behind him. The voices and footsteps moved further and further away down the corridor, submerged beneath the sharp, irritating wails of the maid, who must have entered the bedroom and, finding her mistress's cold body, run out to raise the alarm. Silence settled once more, eventually broken by the timid shuffling of footsteps. Puiu assumed they must belong to his valet, who was probably burning with curiosity. After a while, he heard him in the doorway, summoning the courage to speak:

'Did you call for me, sir?'

Puiu waved him away. The young valet closed the door of the room gently, as if it were the chamber of an invalid.

The silence thickened again, dense, smothering. The grand desk seemed to be disappearing into an exhausting fog. Puiu did not dare make another move. All he could feel, stinging him more and more painfully, was the thought that the old man had still not returned.

It was from him that Puiu now awaited salvation. As for himself, he was not even capable of thought. Besides, his father always knew what to do, made swift and confident decisions, especially at critical times. What horrified him now was that the moments passed so slowly. A gleam of hope bloomed in his heart: if he wasn't coming, maybe Madeleine was not dead after all. . . .

Yet the hope saddened him because he knew it to be senseless and it only reminded him of the deed he was attempting to wipe from his memory.

At last Puiu could no longer bear the quiet. He rose to his feet. He wanted to go, go anywhere, as long as he was no longer alone. Just at that moment his father appeared at the door, followed by Aunt Matilda. Puiu froze by the desk, searching his father with impatient eyes as the old man walked past him without a glance. Instead, Aunt Matilda, bitterly weeping, threw her arms around him in a protective embrace. *'Ah, quel terrible malheur, pauvre petit Puiu!* Poor little Puiu, what a terrible disaster!'

Matilda and Puiu's mother had been sisters. Widowed young and childless, Matilda had shared her heart between her charitable works and her nephew, especially since he had suffered the misfortune of losing his own mother as a very young child. She was now about fifty years old, tall and scraggy, aristocratic, maudlin, constantly chattering.

Faranga cut her off angrily:

'Come now, Matilda, enough! Enough lamentations! Go somewhere else, we've got business to attend to!'

'Mais si, mais si —', murmured Matilda, wiping her eyes. *'Pauvre Madeleine!* Oh the poor girl! What a catastrophe! Look, I'm leaving! Puiu, darling, be strong! Sorrows and misfortunes are sent by God to test us! Stay calm and don't despair, poor little Puişor!'

She embraced him again and kissed him, teary-eyed, on both cheeks.

She turned to leave. From the doorway, she called to the old man, 'And you too, Poly, stay calm, I implore you! And if you need me, call me right away!'

III

Policarp Faranga paced up and down his office, his hands behind his back, his brow bent down towards the floor, while Puiu stayed glued to his spot, observing his father's heavy, pained movements. The whole of the old man's proud, dignified body seemed to have crumpled under the weight of his thoughts.

Never before had Faranga, whose life could hardly have been described as uneventful, received such a sharp and unexpected blow. Since the burden of years had grown heavier upon his shoulders, all of his hopes had been invested in Puiu. Puiu was the sole heir of the Faranga name and fortune, of that ancient boyar family, and was destined to carry on its legacy. There was nothing in the world that gave the old man greater pride than this name. He could trace his ancestors back to Vlad the Impaler. He had found out somehow, and happily repeated this information to anyone who'd listen, that the fearsome ruler had held up a Faranga as an example of honour and loyalty to the other boyars. As centuries passed, the family's wealth had slowly dissipated, but the name remained. . . . Still, old Faranga and his brother had inherited a handsome-enough fortune. But the brother's life had been cut short in his youth and then the name and money became Policarp Faranga's alone.

He married at the age of thirty, having sampled all the compulsory pleasures afforded to a wealthy man with no occupation. Olga Dobrescu, that tender being, was the ideal wife: kindly, beautiful, indulgent, heiress to a fortune. She turned a blind eye to Poly's amorous adventures, which continued after their marriage. Four years later, Puiu was born, and after another four, Olga died. Only after she was gone had Faranga's love for the child begun to take root, alert at last to the boy's significance to the family's future. Around that time the father also put an end to his life of debauchery and entered politics, for something to do.

With his ancestral name and fortune behind him, Faranga's career went from strength to strength. He dabbled in some legal training, but never actually practiced law. The diplomas, however, gave him the right to call himself a barrister. Some friends and well-meaning journalists lauded his oratory style, and somehow he was made a judge. And that was how he became the grave, serious man that he was today. He had grown a magnificent beard after he married and now wore it like a trophy. It had won him a certain celebrity on the boulevards of Bucharest: the finest, best-groomed beard in the whole of Romania. Faranga owed a considerable part of his political gravitas to that beard. Because of a certain popular law that was passed under his watch, he won the esteem of all the legal world and was crowned 'a man of justice'. It had now become inconceivable for anything to be decided at the highest ranks without his consent.

Puiu had grown up swaddled in the idolatrous love of this father, who loved Puiu not only as his child, or as a reminder of the boy's late mother, but as the future of his kin. Faranga loved Puiu because he was part of himself.

The old man was filled with regret over his indolent past, tormented by the thought that the iniquities of the father might be visited upon his son. The boy was fragile, like his mother. And that's why he had to be protected so fiercely. . . .

Pacing automatically around the room, Faranga's mind swarmed with memories and regrets. He stopped for a moment and stared in pity at his son, who was still standing, frozen with clouded anticipation. He whispered gently, 'Sit down, Puiu. . . .'

The youth responded with a questioning look. He sat down.

His father resumed his walk around the room, almost hoping that his mind, retracing their past, could find an answer to their future. . . . All of his attempts to protect the boy had been useless. He had wanted him to marry a girl who would regenerate their ancient blood and give it a new lease of life.

Unions between old families such as theirs produced deficient offspring. When blood was too blue, it started to degenerate. Faranga had married Puiu off early on purpose to protect him from the excesses of his own youth. But Puiu followed in his father's footsteps. Rather than impeding him, marriage stimulated his appetites. And led him into this mess.

Faranga sat down at his desk, calmly, decisively, avoiding Puiu's gaze. The old man remained sunk in thought for a few moments, searching for the right words, and then suddenly picked up the telephone.

'Hello? Yes, put me through to the police station.'

Puiu blanched. The entire reality of the situation bore down on him with that one word. He mumbled, terrified: 'Father, what are you doing?'

'Put me through to the Chief Superintendent.' A minute later: 'Sir? Policarp Faranga here. . . . Yes, it's really me, dear Nicu! No, I haven't left yet and I shan't be going. . . . We were all ready to go and then the most appalling family tragedy. . . . No, no, I'm not exaggerating at all, I repeat, a huge catastrophe! Imagine, my own son, Puiu, in a moment of madness, of course, murdered his own wife. . . .'

The telephone receiver shook in his hand. As he was speaking he held Puiu's gaze, watching his torment as he tried to fathom his thoughts.

'Yes, truly unbelievable. . . . And because of this . . . I pray that you will find it in your heart to come to see me right away, to see what can be done. . . . Please! Of course, I understand that you must bring the prosecutor with you. . . .'

He put the phone down and his hand remained suspended in the air, his eyes fixed on his son.

'You called him here to arrest me?' the young man asked hoarsely, without a drop of colour in his cheeks.

A strange smile played on Faranga's lips.

'You didn't expect any consequences? Nothing at all?'

'Yes. . . . well, yes', Puiu murmured. After a moment, broken, he dropped his head.

'I hope you realise what you've done?'

'I made a mistake', uttered Puiu, in a cracked whisper.

'Come now, you're a murderer!' the old man burst out, as if unearthing the word with the tip of a knife. 'A Faranga, a murderer, like a common thug . . . Ah!'

He crushed a sheet of paper in his fist. More calmly, he added, 'But now there is no time for idle talk. In a few minutes the superintendent will be here. You have until then to decide and to choose!'

Puiu raised his eyes, bewildered:

'Choose what, Father?'

Old Faranga regained his composure, slightly confused.

'Of course, I haven't yet explained . . . I thought that . . .'

He waited a moment for his thoughts to order themselves. Then he got up, drew closer to his son and sat down in an armchair in front of him. He continued in a softened tone, shifting between accusation and pity:

'I haven't asked you a single thing, it's true. . . . I haven't asked why or how you killed her. . . . It would have been pointless anyway. Death speaks louder than words. And yet I cannot help but wonder how any man, let alone my son, could kill someone as good as Madeleine. . . ? Our Mădălina! Who tolerated everything, everything, who didn't even want to hear about all of your senseless, never-ending depravities! It's unbelievable, simply unbelievable!'

'I don't know either, Father', the young man candidly confessed, wringing his hands as he fought back the tears.

'I believe it, I believe it!' Faranga nodded. 'Yes, it must have been a moment's madness, a sudden folly. . . . Only that could make sense of such an inexplicable deed, such a monstrous crime. Because, however depraved you may have been, betraying her with every likely and unlikely woman, I always felt that deep down you truly loved Mădălina. And how could you not love her! Everyone who knew her was enchanted. After all, you chose her, out of love. . . .'

'I loved her a great deal, more than I could tell you, Father.' Puiu's empty eyes seemed to be sinking into the depths of his soul. 'So much, and yet . . .' He fell silent and then, finally, a whisper: 'Perhaps I have lost my mind. . . .'

The old man flinched. Then, almost ashamed of his tenderness, his voice grew harsh:

'All of these are empty words now. The reality is that the superintendent will be here any minute. Crimes must be punished.'

And yet . . .

He hesitated. Perhaps he, too, was still uncertain about what needed to be done.

He groped for words to make sense of his thoughts. 'You must understand that such a deed cannot go unpunished. . . .'

'Would it not be better for me to kill myself, Father?' Puiu suddenly asked, his eyes gleaming.

Faranga glared at him a little contemptuously for a moment.

'That would have been one solution, of course, but it's too late now. Who knows if it might have been for the best? Certainly, it would have made things simpler for me now, but I would have been left without a glimmer of hope. . . . Besides, suicide is spontaneous, like murder. If you couldn't bring yourself to do it then . . .'

His father's irony and his contemptuous gaze hardened Puiu.

'Do you think me a coward?'

'Murderers are usually cowards', Faranga coldly riposted.

The young man, wounded, jumped to his feet, trying to protest.

'Sit down!' his father ordered him. 'Don't try to play the part of the honourable hero, because it never suited you and certainly does not today, of all days. For God's sake, don't you understand?'

'If you can think of nothing better to do than to insult me, in the state that I'm in . . .'

Faranga interrupted with surprising vigour, overwhelmed by pain, his voice soaked in tears:

'Ah, but how you have insulted me with your treacherous deed! You crushed everything, Puiu, everything I thought I had and dreamed of for the future! Policarp Faranga's only son, a common criminal—do you understand what that means for me? And if only your wife had

— 16 —

been wretched, if she had betrayed you or made your days bitter, if . . . But Madeleine was an angel! Everyone knew it. Impossible to think that you could convince anyone that it was a crime of passion, which might be excusable up to a point. No, it's an ordinary crime, odiously, hideously ordinary!'

He stopped to take hold of himself. He was in danger of weeping. Puiu curled himself up in the armchair, feeling through his spine, like an awful pressure, the weight of his deed growing heavier and heavier.

'And yet you are my child and I must save you', Faranga continued, once again in control of his emotions. 'Otherwise they will arrest you, throw you in prison, there will be an investigation, our lives will be torn open, a public trial attended by the press, and they will rummage through our family's intimate secrets. . . . Then the name of Faranga will be forever besmirched and we will be cast out of society—in short, it cannot happen! There remains only one option.'

The young man remained still, stunned by the articulation of the jumbled thoughts that had passed through his own mind and which, uttered by his father's voice, gained an appalling clarity.

'A Faranga cannot be a common criminal', the old man pursued, energetically. 'It cannot be! But if a Faranga were to commit a common crime, he would only do it out of madness! A moment of criminal madness is comprehensible in an ancient family whose stale blood has thickened through time. . . .'

Struggling to understand, Puiu's eyes swam with confusion as he spoke:

'You want to have me committed?'

'I want to save you!' his father insisted. 'Instead of going to prison, you will rest in a hospital, under medical supervision, for a while. Then you will be moved for a few months, let's say, to a good sanatorium, somewhere abroad, and then you will begin a new life, with a name cleared of shame. It will be down to you and only you to prove to the world that the deed you have committed today was an unfortunate folly. . . . And, of course, you will have to wrestle with your demons and make your own peace. Your punishment for robbing poor Mădălina of her life will spring from your own conscience, without any help from me. . . .'

Puiu opened his mouth to say something, but remained frozen in place, as if the muscles of his face had suddenly seized up. The old man waited impatiently for an answer and grew irritated when it finally came as a mild question:

'So you are asking me to choose?'

'Yes', interrupted Faranga. 'Maybe. Or perhaps now I'm advising you, after all, perhaps I don't want to give you the choice. Do as I tell you! Because it is not only your life that's at stake, but mine, all of our lives and the legacy of our ancestors before us. And so . . .'

'And so, I must be mad', Puiu mumbled, dejected, staring beyond his father, into emptiness.

'Better mad than in prison!' came his father's blunt, thundering reply.

There was a long pause. Puiu's voice wavered:

'And if I don't succeed?'

'You must!' ordered Faranga. 'I will deal with this myself. The country owes me that much.'

Once again, they were silent. Questions, doubts and hopes floated through the air, spinning in a suffocating whirl. And then, just as Puiu was about to say something, his valet appeared at the door:

'Sir, the superintendent is here.'

Both men flinched as if waking to an unfamiliar world.

'Very well', said Faranga, himself once more, his voice strained with emotion. 'You wait here', he added to Puiu. 'I'll take them to her. . . . Remember, be brave and have faith! Tidy yourself up before I bring them in.'

He rushed out of the room. His hurried manner ill-suited him and diminished his dignity.

Closing the door, the valet darted a curious, frightened look in Puiu's direction.

IV

'Impossible!' The superintendent crossed himself, then shook Faranga's hand with effusive compassion. 'My dear friend, what a catastrophe! I was just telling the prosecutor about your call and neither of us could believe it. . . . À propos, let me introduce you to Mr Săvulescu, our prosecutor. He's a good lad and truly upset by the whole matter, particularly as you gave the instructions to have him transferred here to Bucharest. . . . '

Faranga shook his hand and barely whispered:

'Let me take you to her room. . . .'

'My commiserations, dear Poly', the superintendent whispered in return, visibly moved.

They stayed there for only a few moments, barely listening to Aunt Matilda's explanations, delivered in a jumble of Romanian and French, punctuated by sobs and calls to the maid—scattered memories of her life and of Puiu and Madeleine's early courtship. Faranga tried to calm her down, but to no avail. The words poured out of her, encouraged by the superintendent's polite flattery and the prosecutor's timid approbation.

Finally, Faranga invited them to step into his office, leaving the maid to deal with Matilda. Seeing them enter the room, Puiu was so horrified that he forgot to stand up. The superintendent walked towards him, shook his hand and spoke loudly, trying to clear the oppressive atmosphere in the room:

'What's all this, Puiu? No, don't get up. I imagine you

must be shattered!' and then, turning to the prosecutor, "Poor boy! What misfortune! You see, that's what they mean by an evil hour, my dear sir!'

Puiu stole a glance at the prosecutor, who seemed too young for his position and too serious for his youth. His eyes were brown, gentle, and calm. He was blond, very shy, and seemed ill at ease. He was still grateful to Faranga, to whom he felt he owed his post, which had in turn enabled him to marry a wealthy young woman.

The youth thought he ought to approach the young Faranga and offer his respects, but the usual introductions had been omitted and besides, he was there in a professional role and couldn't very well fraternise with the accused, even if he was his benefactor's only son.

In stark contrast, the superintendent, Nicolae Spahiu, couldn't stop talking. One of Faranga's oldest childhood friends, he held himself with military erectness (he was indeed a retired colonel) and was reputed to have a heart of gold.

'I was just on my way to the palace when you called', he went on. 'If you had rung five minutes later, you would have missed me.... And I can see that you too were ... They say that as it is the first ball of the season a mere handful of people were invited, only ministers, diplomats, the highest ranking officials, all in all, a very select circle.... But why should we worry now about a palace ball? Oh, God, the poor boy.... These troubles come upon us when we least expect them.... Anyway, back to the matter at hand—we must do our duty! Well, I don't think we have to fill out all these forms.... This is clearly an unfortunate mishap and seeing that it's Faranga's son we are talking about, I think we should wrap up the whole thing as quickly as we can to spare them all unnecessary suffering.... Don't you think so, Mr Prosecutor?'

The prosecutor's eyes searched the faces of all present in the room. He didn't dare disagree, but nor could he bring himself to dismiss such a grave matter with anything like the superintendent's breeziness. It was easy for Spahiu to talk in this way, as he was not responsible for the inquiry, but as for himself . . . Fortunately, Faranga energetically interrupted:

'No, dear Nicu, that's not the solution! Although I agree that this is an unfortunate accident, the law is the law and must be respected! Even though this was no common crime, it doesn't change the fact that a human being died a violent death at the hand of another. . . . Of course, it was a moment's madness, but . . . The first thing that should be done ought to be for the perpetrator to be admitted to an asylum and assessed to see if he is fit to stand trial. After that, we will consider what actions we should take. . . .'

'Precisely, Your Excellency!' the prosecutor burst out with uncharacteristic vigour, relieved.

The superintendent, however, seemed outraged.

'Get away, Poly, don't talk nonsense. Faranga's son in an asylum! You offend me if you insist. . . . Hasn't he suffered enough? Honestly, Poly, the ideas you have! No, I admit, the role of Roman senator suits you, ready to sacrifice your own son out of respect for the law. . . . But don't forget that the days of Roman senators are over and that your gesture would only damage the noblest, most exceptional family in Romania!'

Faranga stood his ground, to the joy of the prosecutor, who had begun to fear that he would become the scapegoat for the whole affair and end up transferred to some forgotten corner of Bessarabia.

Finally, the superintendent was forced to capitulate, still unconvinced yet with begrudging admiration for his friend Faranga's Roman stance. They agreed to admit Puiu to the Demarat de la Şosea sanatorium.

'Bravo!' the superintendent exclaimed. 'To Demarat! Wasn't he in our class at Saint Sava, you must remember him, Poly? I'm sure they'll look after the boy very well there. Good, we're all in agreement!'

The old man offered his car, which was parked outside and was spacious enough for them all.

'Even better!', the superintendent agreed, his cheerfulness by now entirely restored. 'My own car should be in a museum, it's a wreck. . . .'

Puiu had remained silent the whole time, even though the superintendent had been trying to engage him in conversation. Only as they were about to leave did he ask his father's permission to go and change his clothes.

The superintendent offered to wait, but Faranga, keen to get the whole thing over and done with, answered that it was getting late and that he would come by the hospital in the morning and bring him everything he needed.

At the top of the stairs they were met by Matilda, demanding to know how the matter had been settled. Hearing that Puiu would be sent away, she went faint and collapsed in his arms, kissed his cheeks weeping, and declared that it would only be done over her dead body. Faranga was irritated by the scene, thinking that Tilda was embarrassing herself in front of the servants. It took the superintendent's gentle intervention to calm her down:

'*Soyez tranquille, chère madame, tout a fait tranquille!* Do not worry, dear lady! *Ce n'est rien! Une petite formalité, vous savez, enfin, un rien!* It's nothing at all, a formality!'

Gallantly, he kissed her hand and clicked his heels like a valiant sub lieutenant. Matilda was touched. Chivalrous men were her weakness. Still, she shed a few more tears before allowing him to take his leave. The party descended the marble staircase. Upstairs, Matilda continued weeping and incessantly murmuring:

'*Oh, pauvre, pauvre petit Puiu.* Poor, poor little Puiu.'

V

As soon as they found themselves outside the house, old Faranga ordered:

'To the Demarat sanatorium, Alexandru!'

Puiu took the seat behind the chauffeur and the prosecutor sat down beside him. The car started with a gentle jolt. Puiu, himself an accomplished driver, was vexed by the chauffeur's mistake: 'What's got into Alexandru tonight?' he thought to himself, only just managing not to criticise him in front of the others. And then immediately, remembering, he repented: 'But what do I care about these kinds of things now? I must be mad to bother with such trifles while my conscience is burdened with a crime. Perhaps that's why the chauffeur is so nervous too.' In that same moment, he noticed that there was someone else in the car, sitting next to Alexandru.

'Who could it be?' he thought to himself and the question, like an irritating fly, wouldn't go away, especially as everyone in the car had grown silent, as if they were following a funeral procession. Only the engine's muffled, insensible rumble ran on, like an old, placid horse.

The car glided with quiet speed along Colței Boulevard. The afternoon snow had melted into puddles that the wheels splattered into the darkness. The glare of the headlights intertwined with the gleam of occasional streetlights, suspended in the night air. After Piața Victoria, they turned onto the main road and after a few minutes, the car stopped in a quiet side street outside the large iron gate of a house, illuminated by the spotlight of a single lightbulb. Everyone got out of the car except for Puiu, his father signalling to him that he should wait for them there.

'Come on then, ring the bell!' the prosecutor exclaimed impatiently.

A young, slightly alarmed nurse appeared under the spotlight. She exchanged a few words with the prosecutor and then with Faranga. Everyone entered through the gate and the old man approached the car, quietly bidding him:

'You can come out now, Puiu.'

The door had been left open for them. They walked into a clean, wide, warm corridor and listened to their footsteps echoing in the emptiness. To the left, to the right, they could see white doors with black numbers painted on them. They found themselves in a hall where they could see the prosecutor conferring with a blond, lanky young man in a white coat, who was trying hard to be polite and conceal his boredom. All of them now started walking together towards the end of the corridor. Another nun, older, stouter, led the way and opened the door to one of the rooms. Puiu's gaze absorbed the whole cell in an instant. It had a single large, high window with thick iron bars. An iron lavatory, painted white. The bed too was white and made of iron. Between the bed and the window there was a table, pressed against the wall, covered with a white tablecloth, with a floral-patterned mat at its centre; on the mat, a carafe full of water and two glasses. A couple of reed chairs. A narrow wardrobe in the corner, by the window . . .

'This is what we call the "observation room"', said the young doctor, searching the faces of each man in turn, trying to figure out who was destined to inhabit that chamber.

The superintendent paced up and down the cell and finally delivered his verdict, wrinkling his nose:

'It's nothing special, but it will do. . . .'

The junior doctor shrugged his shoulders:

'I'm sorry, gentlemen. . . . That's all we have, that's the best we can do.'

Faranga, muddled and embarrassed, looked around the room while the prosecutor, standing by the door, seemed fixated on the iron bars at the window. The superintendent approached the man in the white coat:

'Listen, young man . . . Do you know who I am? I am the superintendent here and this is Mr Policarp Faranga, the former minister of justice. . . . I'm telling you this so that you treat this patient here with the utmost care and respect, do you understand?'

He pointed to Puiu with a triumphant gesture. The young doctor responded, offended:

'We do our duty here, in all good conscience, sir.'

'Your duty!' the superintendent frowned disdainfully. 'Your "duty" is good enough for the nobodies you pick up from the streets! We're talking here about Mr Faranga's son and you'd better do your best to make him feel at home in this place!'

And without waiting for the man's reply, he turned to Faranga:

'My dear Poly, you must excuse me, I have to go. I need to show my face at the palace, you understand my position. . . . Of course, I'm already terribly late, but for an old friend . . .'

'Yes, of course, . . .' whispered the old man. 'As a matter of fact, it's time for us all to leave. Puiu doesn't need us for the time being. Tomorrow morning I'll come to see him and . . .' He stopped. Hesitated. Then enveloped Puiu in his arms and held him close to his chest for a long time, murmuring:

'*Courage, mon enfant! Sois sage et ... à demain!* Be brave, my child, be good, and I will see you tomorrow!' and then rushed out of the room without looking back.

Visibly moved, the superintendent shook Puiu's hand enthusiastically:

'Be brave, Puiu! Bear it like a soldier and you'll have nothing to worry about!'

Relieved at how things had turned out and no longer afraid of the repercussions that the affair might have for him, the prosecutor rushed to shake young Faranga's hand as well. The young doctor cast his eyes over the room, checking that everything was in order, and then slammed the door behind him. Puiu found himself alone, fixed in his place, without having uttered a word. He remained standing like that for a minute longer, and then took off his hat and coat mechanically and started to walk around the room. He felt as exhausted as if he had been felling trees all day long.

He stopped by the bedside table and looked towards the door. His feet were sore and his head felt as though it were clenched in the jaws of cold pliers. He undressed quickly and got into bed. It was like a swamp had flooded his brain; every scrap of memory began to sink below the surface. The electric lightbulb dangling from the ceiling bothered him. The thought that he should get up and turn it off flashed through his mind. His eyes instinctively scanned the room, searching for the switch, yet he forgot what he was looking for and turned his face towards the wall, closing his eyes. The notion that he had never been able to go to sleep with the light on and the fear that he wouldn't be able to do it tonight, either, floated through his mind. . . . Then he sank into sleep.

VI

Towards the morning, a dream blossomed in his sleep. He was back at home, right there, in Madeleine's boudoir. She was sitting on the sofa in her usual way, with her hands folded in her lap, with that perennial vague look in her eyes, as if she were searching for something in the past. He was in high spirits, chattering to her about nothing in particular, about the ball at the palace, about . . . And, as he was speaking, he drank in her quiet beauty. She had never been as radiant as she was tonight. Her svelte, tender body, like a young girl's, blooming with health, her bare arms, her bewitching décolletage, all of these aroused him. They were waiting for Aunt Tilda to arrive so that they could leave for the palace together. Suddenly he interrupted himself and pleaded, in a whisper:

'Madelon, should we stay at home instead?' She didn't answer. Smiled. A smile as sad as her eyes.

'Madelon, I want you. . . .' He approached her from behind and took her into his arms, then turned her towards him and planted a long kiss between her breasts. Her perfume intoxicated him. A fog crept over his eyes. He murmured tender words under his breath and she laughed gently, avoiding his gaze. . . .

Matilda stormed into the room, puffing and sighing: '*Voyons, mes enfants,* my children, are you ready. . . ? *Il me semble que nous sommes déjà en retard,* we are already late, *oh, mon Dieu!* It took me an age to get ready, my maid is a complete imbecile! And your driver is so slow! *Enfin!* Come downstairs quickly because Poly is waiting for us and he's beginning to lose his patience. . . .' They left together. In the car, he sat next to the chauffeur, to cool off, but his thoughts still lingered in the bedroom, caressing Madeleine's body. . . . The ball was a success. . . . Anyone who was anyone was there. . . . The king himself stopped to talk to Madeleine, his eyes glinting with barely suppressed appetites. Puiu could see those shining royal eyes and his jealousy gnawed at his heart like a tooth ravaged by decay. The music irritated him and especially the men who all seemed to crave Madeleine, sullying her with their greedy looks. He couldn't bear to stay there any longer. He pretended that he had a headache and left with Madeleine, while his father and Aunt Matilda stayed behind. In the car, he pressed her body frenziedly to his chest and kissed her with passion, such passion, wanting to inhale her spirit in one breath. He was dying to get home, but the car moved so slowly, or perhaps the driver had taken the wrong turn.

'What's wrong with you, Alexandru, are you asleep. . . ? Where are you going?' he shouted furiously.

In that moment the car stopped outside an unfamiliar house, in a dark street. The brakes screeched unexpectedly, like a desperate cry. He wanted to get out of the car, angry, but a hand pressed on his shoulder, halting him. Everyone else was to get out first, while he had to wait . . . And then his father summoned him:

'Come now, Puiu, . . .' He left the door open for him. Still turning behind him, towards the car, he murmured: 'But Madeleine . . .' It was cold. A doorbell buzzed sharply.

'In here, in here', his father's voice called to him again. 'Go inside, Puiu!' He couldn't see where he was going and worried that he would hurt himself, bumping into something in the dark. He rubbed his eyes to see more clearly. And, out of the darkness, a large, high window began to take shape, a grey strip of light straining through its bars. The cold dug itself deeper into his bones and the same question kept echoing in his thoughts: 'But Madeleine?' And then, finally coming awake, he told himself with certainty: 'Madeleine could not have been in the car....' He noticed that the lightbulb was off. 'It must be morning, the doctor is going to find me in bed.... Quickly, up, up!' On the nightstand he could see the change from his trouser pockets, a notebook with a gold pencil, keys, a handkerchief, a slim wallet, his platinum watch with the cover open....

He looked at the watch: seven o'clock.... He started to get dressed. He had gone to sleep in his shirt and it was as crumpled as a rag.

'Why does it matter?' he consoled himself. 'Never mind my shirt, I mustn't lose my mind!'

VII

He paced, restlessly, from the nightstand to the window, the window to the nightstand, like a wolf in a cage. He had ample time to familiarise himself with that cell that would be his home for a week, maybe a month, if not longer. He paused for a long time in front of the window, looking out at the garden of the sanatorium, a small patch of land bordered by trees through which he could distinguish a barbed wire fence, making escape impossible. The pathways, almost entirely covered in snow, snaked their way through some dreary shrubbery. Then, as he continued wandering through the room, he discovered a bowl of dirty water and washed himself quickly, drying himself with a crumpled towel. He could see on the bed the crushed pillow and the covers in disarray and remembered kicking them off in the night, under the spell of his disturbing dream. He noticed his overcoat hanging in the empty wardrobe, with his top hat directly above it, shiny and new, at a slightly jaunty angle, mockingly, like the crown of a drunkard.

But then, pacing up and down, he stopped noticing anything at all. His whole attention concentrated inward. Thousands of thoughts and plans roved through his mind, swarming around—unendingly, tediously—spurred on by the dream that had woken him from his sleep. He wanted, beyond anything else, to gain back control over these thoughts, otherwise he knew that all the old man's careful calculations would come crashing down like a house of cards. It would be appalling if his plans came to nothing. Everyone would rightly surmise that Puiu Faranga, after murdering his wife, had been so cowardly that he tried to feign madness to avoid the consequences of his crime.

The enormity of his undertaking began to dawn on him. Easy for his father to say 'pretend to be mad'—but who would believe him? He knew that from his very first meeting with the doctor he must create an image of himself as a man who had indeed committed a serious crime but who could not be held accountable for it as it had been borne out of a moment of extreme confusion and thus deserved mercy and forgiveness. How could he begin to fool the doctor, when he hadn't even so much as encountered a madman in his entire life? If only he had read something about such things beforehand! But who would have imagined that Puiu Faranga would find himself in a situation like this, under observation in an asylum? All he could do was to place all his hope in the doctor's benevolence. Of course, he had to play his part, to give him a helping hand. . . . He found himself again by the window, his eyes searching the garden outside for the tenth time. The idea crossed his mind that he should bang on the window with his fists, to alarm everyone. . . . Would that be the right kind of thing to do. . . ? He discarded the idea disdainfully: 'A ridiculous gesture, no doubt. . . . It would be obvious I was putting it on!' He couldn't feign a true and permanent lunacy, he had to convince them that all that had happened had been due to one ill-fated moment. His performance had to be more subtle, almost imperceptible, a madness that betrayed itself only through hints of disturbance or an unsettled demeanour.

In any case, everything was riding on that first meeting. He tried therefore to imagine it, almost to plan it.

He was sure that once the doctor heard his name he would be shocked or would smile amiably or try to comfort him. He could almost hear him asking: 'But how could this happen? You, the son of Faranga, the former minister!' And then he would undoubtedly ask him for a detailed account of the tragic events. . . .

He began to concoct a story where reality merged with small peculiarities that would help the doctor reach his diagnosis. At last, the medic would shake his head and conclude, sadly: 'Nerves, my dear sir, nerves need to be looked after carefully!' But just at that moment he could hear his own voice, taking him by surprise, echoing the question lingering from his dream: 'But Madeleine. . . ?' He recoiled in shock, startled by the touch of a spectre from another world. He didn't want to think of her now, even though her name whirled around his soul unendingly, like a quiet remonstrance. Why should he still think of her? She was at peace now. Death had smoothed over all her fears and sorrows. Whereas his life, on which so much depended, how ugly and tortured it promised to be! If only he had had the courage to follow her to the other side last night, he wouldn't have had to wait, full of anxiety and shame, for the arrival of the doctor!

He flinched. Voices were coming from the hall. Frozen, he stopped by the bed. The door opened noiselessly.

VIII

'And you are?'

'My name is Puiu Faranga and I was brought here last night because . . .'

He hesitated for a second. He met the doctor's eyes and found them filled with a disconcerting indifference. Nevertheless, he carried on in the same bland tone:

'. . . because I strangled my wife.'

The doctor didn't even blink, as if he hadn't heard him. He was clearly listening, while at the same time looking him straight in the eye and then noticing his messy hair, his odd clothing—the dinner jacket, the crumpled shirt, the white cravat that he had put on crooked without the aid of a mirror, the patent shoes . . . After a couple of moments he took in the unmade bed, the evidence of a restless sleep, and frowned vaguely.

The junior doctor, who had noticed his expression, intervened immediately:

'I had been told to await your instructions so that is why . . .'

Attempting a slightly inappropriate smile, Puiu Faranga offered:

'I had to come straight away in what I was wearing. They were supposed to come to bring me a change of clothes and I'm surprised they haven't arrived yet. But I expect that my father, who I'm sure you must have heard of, will bring them himself. . . .'

'Fine!' the doctor muttered curtly, looking him up and

down again as if he hadn't heard a word he said or as if none of it interested him. Yet for a second he appeared to want to ask him something, but then suddenly turned around and walked out, followed by the deferential blond doctor.

Through the half-open door he could see the guard, a heavyset figure with curly black hair, an impressive moustache, and shiny, beady eyes. Then the thick, rough green glass door slid shut with a click of the lock. A round viewing hole shone in its centre like a watchful yellow eye.

Puiu remained frozen in place, looking incredulously at the door. He'd only just noticed the fact that the door was made of glass and that it slid open and shut, without a door handle, like the door of a prison cell. . . . Outside he could hear the murmur of low voices, coming from the guard's room. He tiptoed to the door and pressed his ear against it, holding his breath. He couldn't make out anything except indistinct mumbling. Moments later, the noise faded away. The footsteps of the doctors echoed faintly down the corridor and the guard must have been left alone with his thoughts, unless he had followed them out too.

'They must have been talking about me!' Puiu told himself, returning to the centre of the room as if he was still waiting for something. The complete silence forced him to come to his senses, and he was immediately overcome by despair. All the plans and fantasies with which he had furnished this meeting in his imagination had turned to dust in one stroke. A burning doubt pierced his heart: 'What if Father was wrong to send me here? What if the doctor is harsh and unyielding?' He resumed pacing around the room just as before the doctor's visit, angry and miserable. He had the feeling that the whole room was swirling around him. The thoughts that had preyed on him while he was anticipating this meeting overwhelmed him again. Yet while everything then had seemed to take on a rosy, hopeful glow, now the future seemed dark and full of peril.

'And how beautifully I had planned everything!' he told himself, stopping in the same place as before.

He closed his eyes and again saw the doctor, cold, apathetic and glum.

'He's got the face of a stubborn peasant—muttering between his teeth and wandering around the room. I don't know how the old man could ever conceive of locking me away in here, in this hole. Or could it be that this man wasn't really the doctor? It could be. He looked too young and too rough to be a real doctor.'

He remembered that he had actually not been properly welcomed from the very beginning. The junior doctor had been so slow that the superintendent had chastised him. It seemed that he hadn't appreciated the significance of having such a distinguished patient in his care. When they parted, all of them had been moved, even the prosecutor, who was a stranger to him; only the junior doctor had stood there inert, like a drowsy imbecile. But surely, he, Puiu Faranga, shouldn't waste his energy caring about the indelicacy of a junior doctor who ought to have been flattered that a Faranga had deigned to shake his hand. Last night he hadn't even given it a second thought.

His spirits were utterly crushed. He, who in thirty years had not committed a single brutal act, his well-groomed, manicured hands soft like a woman's, those hands had been capable of . . . He shuddered and, suddenly aware of his hands clenched behind his back, opened them, almost looked at them, but then immediately changed his mind and hid them in his trouser pockets.

He was as rattled as a car whose brakes had snapped.

New plans began to form in his mind. He swatted them away. What was the point of plans, when he had no control over anything anyway, when he was reduced to a broken plaything, discarded by his father to rot away between these four walls? His fury began to sharpen against the old man because he had encouraged, no, he had ordered him to come here. . . .

He heard a new voice calling out to him:

'The doctor will see you now.'

He hadn't heard the door open. It was the guard, in his ill-fitting uniform, wearing the shifty expression of a spy. Puiu stared at him for a second, then exhaled, relieved, rushing out of the room as if he were abandoning it forever. In the corridor, the junior doctor was waiting to take him to the consultation room.

IX

The doctor signalled to the junior doctor to leave them alone. With exaggerated politeness, he offered the patient an armchair and drew his chair nearer to observe him closely.

'I'd like us to have a little talk,' he said in a formal tone as he sat down, his voice neither cordial nor antagonistic. 'I have been briefed about . . . your situation, of course, to some extent. I know the bare facts of the matter. . . . Yet you must be aware that what I've been told is insufficient for me to reach any conclusions and that it would be in your interest to fill in some details for me. . . .'

As he was talking, he was fixing Puiu with his eyes, unsettling him, so that he couldn't tell whether it would be better to hold the doctor's stare or to avoid it. He rushed to answer politely and with genuine sorrow in his voice:

'I am, of course, entirely at your disposal, Doctor! I promise that I will be honest about everything you want to ask me, no matter how delicate. After everything that's happened I understand that every detail could be important and all must be revealed. . . .'

He fancied that he saw a tremor of mockery shifting through the doctor's face. Even though he was about to add something about how certain misfortunes come upon us in an evil hour, he stopped himself, concluding that this man did not deserve his candour. The doctor, however, waited calmly for another couple of moments, staring at him fixedly as before, and when he saw that the pause was lasting too long, he continued in the same neutral tone:

'Just now, I've received some information about your case. . . . I've been told that you have been accused of murder and that there is a question as to whether you committed the crime during a nervous breakdown, thus making it necessary for you to have a psychiatric assessment so that the extent to which you can be held accountable for this crime can be legally determined.'

Wanting to observe the effect of his words on his patient, the doctor fell silent. Puiu listened with visible concentration, blinking rapidly. The doctor added in a grave tone:

'Therefore I felt I needed to inform you of this, in case you were not aware that you are under observation and in fact in custody, to all intents and purposes, although not officially.'

Puiu stood up suddenly, perturbed, wanting to protest. Then he sat down again and mumbled confusedly:

'I wasn't aware of that. They had told me that . . . So, actually under arrest? Well, I thought . . . So the guard outside my room. . . ?'

'Yes, he's a police officer', the doctor assented, nodding his head. 'As this is a private sanatorium, it wouldn't have been appropriate for us to harbour a suspect without involving the authorities. For these kinds of things, the justice system has its own procedures and its own institutions. But as this is a special case, I have permitted a police officer to keep guard by your room, instead of the usual nurses. This is why I have to warn you that you cannot leave your room except when accompanied by your guard.'

'Oh, in that respect, there is no need to warn me, I

have gathered that already!' exclaimed Puiu with a disdain that immediately embarrassed him, so that he added in a more placatory tone: 'Besides, my situation is so deplorable, so . . .'

The doctor shrugged his shoulders. Puiu, encouraged by this gesture, changed his tone once again:

'Can you tell me at least, doctor, how long these observations will last?'

The doctor smiled:

'How should I know? It depends on the circumstances: a week, maybe two . . . six at most. If I can reach a diagnosis before that—and this will depend on you—then we might resolve this sooner! In any case, I have no desire or interest to drag things out any longer than necessary.' And then, in a different tone: 'But let's go back to our original discussion. At the moment all I know is that you killed your wife. Do you want to tell me more about how and, more importantly, why you did it? Please don't be surprised by my prying into your private affairs. Even though I'm not a judge, I need to know the particulars of the case and weigh up the evidence.'

Puiu coughed, feeling ill at ease. He had been dreading this moment, the moment of explanations, and now it was here. He began in a pleading voice:

'Yes, of course, doctor, but I choke on the answers to your questions just as I am about to utter them and I struggle to find the words. I can't find the strength to answer you!'

The doctor calmly insisted:

'We will find the answers together, we must . . . Let's reconstruct the events as clearly as possible.'

'Yes, doctor, yes', Puiu murmured, like a child subdued after a fit of rebellion. 'But that dreadful night has all but dissolved in my memory! Everything happened only in a few moments, doctor, truly, in mere moments. . . . And I was so lost, so . . .'

'Had you had a disagreement, a row?' the doctor asked.

'No, doctor', Puiu cut in quickly. 'No! And that's the most frightening thing! But why do you go on, doctor? Please. I beg you. . . . I will tell you everything. . . . I want to tell you. . . . It would lift this burden from my soul. . . . But I don't know. . . . We were getting ready to go to the ball at the palace. We had finished dressing. As you can see, I'm still wearing . . . Madeleine was silent, as always. I asked her something, I can't remember what. She did not answer. I repeated the question and she looked at me like she wasn't really there. There was no malice in that look, nothing that should have provoked me, only an absence, and yet I felt overwhelmed by this fury, I remember, like something I have never felt before. There was a roar in my ears and it seemed to me that she was screaming and insulting me, I don't know why. . . . At the same time I could tell that she was actually silent, that she hadn't uttered a word, that she was merely looking at me, with a tinge of disapproval. . . . anyway . . . Perhaps that look in her eyes had transformed itself in my soul into that scream that kept echoing in my ears, I don't know, how can I know. . . . And then I could no longer bear that scream and I lunged at her. . . . I wanted to stifle that scream before it pierced my eardrums or maybe . . . And she, aghast, didn't even move or try to defend herself. If she had tried to defend herself, I'm sure that I would have come to my senses and this tragedy wouldn't have happened. . . . But she did nothing at all and this only made my fury swell and . . . and . . . the fury . . . the fury . . .' He became tongue-tied. He could not go on. He burst into hysterical sobs, without tears, with painful, frequent shudders.

The doctor waited for him to calm down, then continued amiably:

'I had the honour of being introduced to your wife once, at a charity ball. The lady probably would not have remembered my name, and you were not there that night. . . . A very beautiful woman. That's not my opinion, it was the general consensus about her in society. . . . So perhaps . . .'

Puiu flinched as if after a blow:

'Oh no, doctor, I must stop you there! I won't tolerate any word that might besmirch her memory, not even a suggestion of such a thing! Madeleine was the most faithful woman in the world. Like any man, I have sinned, but she only repaid me with loyalty. She was too good, too tolerant, that's why. . . .'

Unperturbed, the doctor continued:

'I certainly wasn't hinting at any betrayal on her part! The question related only to you. . . . I mean, might it be possible that a woman so beautiful and, I assume, so admired, could stir in your heart the kind of jealousy, at least on a subconscious level, that might have exploded in the events of last night? That's all I meant to ask!'

Puiu settled down right away. The doctor's theory provided a justification that he had not considered himself. A subconscious emotion that erupted without a warning, unheeded, that could excuse everything! He wanted to agree but in the moment when he was about to utter the words, he fell dumb. It seemed to him too shameful a lie and not worthy of him. Instead, he answered quietly:

'No, no, nothing like that! Me, jealous? I, who betrayed her, without an ounce of shame, with women not worthy even of kissing her feet? You see, doctor, I do not try to hide anything from you, not one of my sins! No, it wasn't jealousy, for better or worse, that was not the motive!'

The doctor fell quiet. He began examining his fingers for a while. Then he sat up quickly:

'I don't want to tire you out today. You are already agitated. We will talk about all of this in due time, properly. Try to calm down. Here, you will have complete peace and I'm sure that you will manage to relax a little, you'll see. . . .'

He must have rung the bell without Puiu noticing. The junior doctor was suddenly at the door.

'Please take this gentleman to his room', said the doctor, then turning towards Puiu: 'Good-bye!'

The guard was waiting for him in the corridor. Closing the door behind him, the junior doctor whispered to the doctor:

'Mr Faranga is here. . . . He's coming over right now! He wants to talk to you.'

The old man, red-eyed, was embracing his child:

'I've brought you everything you need! The valet has put it all in your room. . . . Courage, *mon enfant*, courage! I'm coming to see you right away, I just need to have a little chat with our friend, the doctor!'

Meanwhile, the junior doctor had announced his visit and was showing him in.

'*À tantôt!* See you in a minute!', murmured Faranga with a forced smile, and disappeared inside.

Puiu brightened, as if released from all his troubles. He led the way, smiling at the guard who followed him like a sinister shadow.

X

The room no longer seemed gloomy to him. He rubbed his hands together, almost cheerful, not even noticing that the door had been locked behind him. In his absence, someone had cleaned and tidied his room and on his bed he found, neatly arranged, his clothes and toiletries.

'Very good, very good', he murmured, looking at them with satisfaction. 'Before anything else, I should make myself look presentable.' As he was getting dressed, he replayed the encounter with the doctor and deemed it satisfactory. The man hadn't seemed as hostile as he had at their first meeting. Certainly, there was something enigmatic about him, a certain slyness hiding behind the eyes that betrayed his rustic origins—that's why he gave the impression of being a sneaky, dubious type. But still, he couldn't deny that he had acted towards him in an honest and dignified manner.

'Putting on an act doesn't fool people like that', Puiu told himself, satisfied. 'It would have been so embarrassing if I had started to pretend!' He was glad that he hadn't exaggerated the story of the tragic event in the way that he had planned it out that morning. The truth and nothing but the truth, that was the only way. . . . At the end of the day, he would not have been capable of lying and thus burdening his conscience even further. What he really needed was relief, and the lie could only complicate the situation unnecessarily and make him feel disgusted with himself. This was why, when he had been asked about jealousy, he had refused to lie, even though it might have seemed convenient at the time to go along with the theory. Come to think of it, the doctor's question about that was a little insolent! Anyway, none of it really mattered. Since there was nothing left to do for poor Madeleine, at least he could be saved from the ordeal fate had prepared for him. It wasn't the doctor's questions that mattered, but his intentions. In that respect, however, the doctor was a sphinx. He wasn't expecting much from him. Up until now, in any case, he had been treating him as if he were a nobody, if not worse. He had implied that his presence was not welcome there, that it could damage the reputation of the sanatorium.

'The old man was wrong to send me here', Puiu reflected, feeling increasingly gloomy. 'His impulsive decision is going to be the end of me. He should never have delivered me into the hands of a stranger, and a hostile one at that.' He replayed in his mind the doctor's words and gestures, discovering in each of them the shadow of a hidden animosity. He even figured out the motive: from the story he had told about meeting Madeleine, he could detect now, recalling his tone, evidence of a secret passion.

Of course, he would have only loved her from afar, as Madeleine, with her refined nature, would never have stooped to the level of this doctor who was neither handsome nor intelligent, not even charming. On the other hand, it would have been natural for him to be infatuated with her. And these were the most dangerous kinds of passions. A lover hiding in the shadows, unknown, would be capable of the lowest of blows when seeking his revenge.

'Unbelievable!' Puiu crossed himself. 'My fate is in the

hands of an enemy!' He felt overcome by a suffocating impatience. He needed to escape from there straight away, to move to another sanatorium, at least to find himself in the care of a man with no vengeful intentions. He was convinced that the doctor was his rival and wished to condemn him to death.

'And what's keeping my father?' he sighed miserably.

He turned towards the door. Only then did he realise it was locked. He charged at it and began pounding at the thick glass.

'Why did you lock me in?' he snapped at the guard, who immediately opened it.

'We have been given orders and I had to, . . .', the frightened man responded, with a certain deference.

'I don't want you to lock this door unless I order you to!' shouted Puiu. 'I need air, do you understand? I'm going to suffocate in this cage!'

Old Faranga appeared at the door:

'*Qu'est-ce qu'il y a, Puiule?* What's the matter, my boy. . . ? *Soyons calmes, voyons!* Come now, let's stay calm. . . . Come inside, we need to talk. . . .'

Puiu threw a contemptuous gaze towards the guard:

'This idiot irritates me!' And then, moving back inside, he added: 'Yes, you can shut it now, you fool, you can shut it now!'

XI

'Leave it, Puiu, dear boy, don't get angry!' murmured Faranga with a mild smile shimmering with pain. He hung his fur coat and hat on the coat hanger and then wiped his forehead with his handkerchief, looking around the room:

'You know, Puiu, this isn't too bad. Almost cosy, . . .' he said, indicating that his son should sit on the bed and himself taking the chair beside it. He watched him cautiously, his eyes full of pity. He informed him that after he had left him the previous evening he had found out that Professor Demarat was not in Bucharest. The doctor had just confirmed that he would be away for another three months. He had been sent by the government to Germany, on some business or other. . . . It had been in the papers, he remembered reading about it now, but yesterday it had slipped his mind! He had been gone for over a week.

'The fact that he's not here makes no difference, of course,' the old man added, with an air of authority designed to convince his son. 'His replacement will serve us just as well!'

In truth, the old man was very anxious. His old school friend would have treated the whole matter differently: Faranga would have asked for his help and the man would have unquestioningly given it. The young doctor didn't particularly impress him, but because he wanted to hide his doubts from Puiu, he began to sing his praises:

'He seems like a decent sort. . . . I made some enquiries about him and he comes highly recommended. He is a well-respected doctor, Demarat's assistant at the university and his natural successor. In fact, they say that even when the professor is here Ursu effectively runs the sanatorium. Oh, yes, I nearly forgot: his name is Ion Ursu and he's the son of a peasant. Very honourable and very conscientious; his only fault is that he is a little gauche, a little prickly, so he doesn't make a good first impression, until you get to know him better.'

Puiu, desperate for any comfort, cast out of his mind his earlier suspicions and hungrily lapped up the old man's reassurances. When he had heard that the doctor, without making any definite promises, had implied that he wanted to resolve the matter quickly and seemed to be of the opinion that the tragedy had been the result of a mental breakdown, he seemed visibly cheered and interrupted excitedly:

'So you mean, you think there is hope, Father? Do you really think so?'

'How can you doubt it?' answered Faranga, touched by his despair, tears welling up in his eyes. 'You just need to be patient. You will need to be very, very patient, Puiu! What can I say? When you suffer such a painful blow, you must endure it with dignity.'

Puiu asked him to repeat again every detail of the meeting with the doctor. The old man willingly acquiesced, taking care to embroider everything that could be an omen of hope and keep quiet about any concerns.

'And you know, Father, I couldn't bring myself to dissemble at all!' said Puiu. 'I don't even think I could have known how to do it. It's just not in my nature and my soul is burdened enough already. I can't seem to keep at bay the thought that I should just confess to it all, just like that. What do you think?'

'Calm down, Puiu, don't get carried away!' said the old man soothingly. 'We must consider our position. You have been punished enough by your conscience, you have paid the price in your own way. Don't worry, when it comes to it, I will make sure that things go smoothly, as they should! But for now, dear Puiu, I can't stay here any longer. I have duties relating to Madeleine. . . .'

The young man bowed his head and assented with a heartfelt cry:

'You're right, Father, you're right! Oh God, I am a selfish bastard!'

Anxious to soothe him, Faranga brought the conversation back to the doctor and told him that the medic had granted him as much freedom as possible: he could read what he wanted, enjoy himself however he wished, receive guests when he was calm enough, walk in the gardens accompanied by the guard. . . . He could eat whatever he wanted, without any restrictions, the papers would be brought to him. . . . In summary, he could make himself at home. The old man had suggested sending his servant there, but the doctor had said that this would break the rules of the sanatorium. ('He will need to be content with the services of the guard, who will attend to his every need.')

'I hope that Matilda has sent you everything you wanted? I confess that I didn't have time to check. If there is anything missing, ask them to ring me, or ring me yourself. . . . In any case, I shall visit you every day, unless something unexpected happens. . . . Poor Tilda was devastated and burst out crying when I told her that I wouldn't bring her to see you. Well, it simply wasn't possible. Someone had to stay with Madeleine, didn't they?'

'I'm so sad, Father, that I can't be at the funeral!' Puiu suddenly sighed, his misery returning. Faranga was moved and decided that, after all, Puiu was a good boy with a wonderful heart. He had made a serious mistake, of course, but not out of malice, as was clear from the immense and sincere regret that spontaneously erupted from his soul.

'You've got to just think of yourself now,' the old man said to him, enveloping him in a gaze filled with endless love.

He told him all the news from home. He complained that he had been struggling to keep the reporters at bay, trying to keep the attention off the case. Of course, he had no intention of burying the news, but he didn't want them to exaggerate anything, to turn it into a scandal. The superintendent, having a certain influence with the media, promised to help him out, although he thought it would be prudent to put in a word with the minister for internal affairs, just in case.

However, he quickly noticed that Puiu didn't seem interested in any of these things. He too fell silent. It dawned on them both that they had nothing more to say to each other. Before long, Faranga rose to his feet, getting ready to leave, half hoping that Puiu might try to stop him.

'You have no idea how much there is still left to do. . . .'

Silently, Puiu helped him put on his coat.

XII

He felt calmer once he was alone again. It wasn't the guard who had shut the door this time—he asked him to lock it.

He lay on his bed for a long time, his eyes fixed on the ceiling. He was constantly on the verge of tears. A heavy burden seemed to weigh on his chest, yet he almost enjoyed the sensation. The silence in the room was so complete that he sunk into it as into a hot, comforting bath. He imagined that instead of lying in bed, his body was raised on a catafalque, and he savoured the illusion that through death he had escaped from all his troubles. Eventually, he gave up on the fantasy, bored.

Rising from the bed, he felt at once overwhelmed by fatigue. He drew the chair that his father had sat on earlier towards the window. The pure white snow in the garden stilled his heart. He waited there until dinnertime, when the guard arrived with his tray of food.

'I'm not hungry,' Puiu muttered softly. 'Eat it yourself!'

The man hesitated. He wanted to insist but didn't dare. Meanwhile, Puiu had turned back towards the window, and eventually the guard left the room, closing the door behind him.

He sat in the same position for several hours, paralysed, his mind as hollow as a dry sponge. Occasionally, as his body shifted, the chair scraped the floor, but the sound was immediately swallowed up by the silence, as blank as the snow in the garden.

Outside, it began to snow again, large, languorous snowflakes like white butterflies floating down from the sky. The branches of the trees sagged as if heaving with fruit ready for harvest. Veils of snow rippled from the surrounding wall, thickening, collapsing. . . .

Puiu felt at peace, his mind empty. The time flooded over him like a stream, in a long, hypnotic murmur. His eyes absorbed only the silent white that melted the roots of his thoughts, like bubbles dissolving on the mirror-like surface of a lake. And yet, after a while, a door in his soul had opened out to the past and he suddenly saw himself, two weeks ago, standing just like this, at a window, in a hotel room in Sinaia, watching the winter's early snow. It was the day of the ladies' skiing contest. He was there purely for the sake of Miss Lia Dandopol, the very modern, sporty and wanton daughter of a nouveau-riche businessman, who, after a month of his relentless pursuit, was finally giving him reason to hope.

Having won the contest, she capitulated to Puiu and now, as she rested in bed, naked and exhausted by sport and love, he, haunted by regrets he couldn't swat away, disgusted with himself, returned in his thoughts to Madeleine, at home. . . . He felt guilty and sullied. She had begged him to take her to the skiing contest but he had refused—the only time she had begged him for anything. And he had refused. He lied that he had some urgent business in Cluj and it wouldn't be possible. He was so adamant, if not brutal, in his refusal, that she did not insist. And now he was sorry and missed Madeleine. . . .

And then, as if through a kaleidoscope, all the snow-filled scenes of his life flickered through his memory. He saw himself as a five-year-old child, in a white woolen snowsuit, bundled up to the tip of his nose, riding on a small sleigh attached to a large one, where Aunt Tilda sat and turned to him, smiling encouragingly, yet frightened should her precious boy come to any harm, while the precious boy let out an Indian war cry, half joyful, half terrified, that echoed through the street.... All of them gathered around the Christmas tree, in Aunt Matilda's grand drawing room, celebrating Puiu's first year at school. A huge Christmas tree, surrounded by others of a more modest size, all of them laden with artificial snow and lights, like a forest on fire.... The floor covered with artificial snow and presents for him and all his school friends. And the snow kept falling inside.... Aunt Tilda never explained this miracle to him.... Evening, in Cişmigiu Park. Sitting on a bench, now in sixth grade, next to a girl with a snub nose and the eyes of a squirrel—his first love. Above the bench, the canopy of an ancient tree. He had chosen this spot because he thought it romantic and had cleared the snow from the bench before she arrived. They held each other close, snug and warm, and he could not stop kissing her eyes and her mouth, his lips feverish, her eyes frozen. From time to time a branch scattered snow on them and they laughed.... And now he is a second lieutenant, during the war, loosely engaged in some clerical duties because his father was determined to shelter him from the danger of battle. Păcurari Street, in Iaşi, in a cramped room plastered with photographs, a warm stove, sunset.... He is sitting in a wide, threadbare armchair, bouncing Adina Fulgeru on his lap, a young, passionate actress with whom he had begun an affair and on whom he had spent a fortune entertaining, appalling his father. She was wearing a short silk chemise, pulled up high and his hands gripped her naked hips. Her arms slack around his neck, her cheek pressed to his, they listened to each other's breathing and watched in silence the grimy street where creaky carriages carried the corpses of those who had died of fever as the snow kept falling. Whenever he lowered his eyes, his gaze fell on her bare white breasts, full and soft, as their intoxicating perfume compelled him to bury his nose in them, tickling her, until she, with her neck stretched back and her chin up in the air, burst out in irresistible giggles. . . .

The door suddenly opened noisily. Puiu flinched, startled by the noise, as if he had been caught with the actress still in his lap. The junior doctor asked him quickly:

'Do you need anything?'

'Nothing,' Puiu responded, turning his head towards him without getting up.

'If you prefer, we can keep the door open—' the doctor continued obliviously, at the same speed. 'You would get more air and the air . . .'

'Yes-' Puiu interrupted coldly, his face turned back to the window.

The junior doctor fell quiet, but loitered for a couple of moments, looking like he was about to say something. Eventually, he went out of the room, leaving the door open. Puiu heard him say something to the guard. He rose quickly to his feet. He stopped himself from walking to the door and instead started pacing around the room, to wake up his stiff bones. The guard appeared at the door:

'I brought you the newspapers. . . .'

'What newspapers? Who asked you to bring them to me?' Puiu asked suspiciously.

'The distinguished older gentleman ordered me to bring you newspapers every morning and every evening, to keep you entertained', said the guard.

'Alright, alright', murmured Puiu, resuming his walk around the room.

After the guard put the newspapers on the bedside table, he retreated towards the door, and at the last moment asked him again:

'The doctor has asked me to find out what you normally like to eat at teatime and to bring you whatever you wish. . . .'

Puiu turned to face him and answered dejectedly:

'Why can't you leave me alone, boy?'

Touched by his sorrow, the guard whispered humbly:

'Yes, sir, I'm just following orders. Please forgive me. . . .'

His sincerity moved Puiu who, after a few more steps around the room, approached him and patted him on the shoulder companionably:

'It's alright. . . . you see, I'm a little nervous. . . . Look, bring me a cup of tea, but see to it that it's very hot!'

'Of course, sir, right away,' the guard answered quickly, immediately brightening. 'It is good to eat while you are grieving, otherwise the grief will eat *you* up and destroy you.' He left with a cheerful expression on his face. Puiu also felt brighter. He picked up a newspaper and cast his eyes over the headlines. On the front page: 'Conjugal murder in high society'. He dropped the paper, muttering:

'I don't want to know anything. . . . I'm not interested in anything. . . .'

XIII

Sipping his tea, Puiu could not take his eyes off the guard, who stood by the door, radiant, satisfied, convinced that his presence there would cheer up the patient and ease his loneliness. The man's discreet, humble pity filled Puiu with wonder and was more soothing than his father's attempts to console him. Here was a simple man, a stranger, who understood his suffering and tried his best to alleviate it. Up until now, the only relationship that he had ever had with a man of this type had been that of a master and servant. He had never had a conversation with someone like him and had never imagined such a man to be capable of fine feelings.

In order to show his gratitude, he inquired in a friendly tone:

'What's your name, boy?'

'Andrei Leahu, sir', the guard eagerly responded.

'And where are you from?' Puiu continued. 'What county?'

'From Argeş, sir, a place called Ciofrângeni.'

'Argeş?' Puiu reacted, a little perturbed. 'I have spent some time in Argeş. An uncle, on my mother's side, owned an estate in Măneşti.'

'I wouldn't be surprised,' agreed the guard. 'There are many boyar estates in those parts. Even where I'm from, Ciofrângeni, there were two, but now only one is owned by a boyar. The other one died in the war and his wife sold up and moved to the city, to Piteşti. The peasants bought the land from her. . . .'

After a moment's pause, compelled by an overpowering memory, Puiu eagerly asked:

'And do you know the Ciuleandra, in those parts?'

'Ciuleandra?' Leahu smiled. 'Of course we know it, sir. But we call it Suleandra, where I'm from. It really is a wonderful dance', he added. 'Once you start it, you don't want to stop. . . . Have you ever danced the Suleandra, sir?'

'Yes. . . . I mean . . .' Puiu stuttered, taken aback by the question, suddenly regretting having opened the subject of the Ciuleandra.

The guard sensed the gentleman's embarrassment and fell silent, especially as he noticed that he had stopped eating and reasoned that he must have been feeling awkward on account of his presence. It crossed his mind that he should quietly retreat and leave him alone to eat in peace. Puiu, however, changed his plan with another question:

'When did they send you here? Last night?'

'Last night, sir', Andrei Leahu confirmed. 'I came in the same car as you, I was sat in the front, next to the driver, when they brought you here. . . . The superintendent brought me along, in case I was needed. Then, once they settled you in here, just as we were about to leave, the two gentlemen, the superintendent and your father, made some arrangements and asked the doctor to bring me a white coat straight away and told me that I was to stay here and look after you. . . .'

Puiu remembered how he had wondered the night before who the man was sitting next to the chauffeur, and immediately asked:

'So, does that mean you know why I'm here?'

'How could I not know, sir?' the guard said, shaking his head sympathetically. 'That's how misfortune gets you, it watches you and watches you until it gets you, God is my witness!' He bowed piously. 'Yes, of course, I've heard all about it!'

Intrigued to find out this simple man's opinion of his deed, Puiu insisted:

'Well, but why do you think they brought me here to hospital instead of . . .'

He stopped, not daring to ask the question. Nevertheless, Leahu understood and answered jovially:

'Sure, they couldn't very well jail you with all the thieves and common criminals, I'll say! It would have been a scandal. . . . But God willing, you will get out of here soon. In cases like this, the jury always forgives crimes of passion.'

He looked directly into his eyes, watching his reaction, ready to change the subject if he seemed offended. Yet the young man was comforted by his words and nodded slowly as he listened to him:

'Yes. . . . yes. . . . yes. . . .'

Then, after a considerable pause, he looked him up and down with affection and teased him amiably:

'I see that you're a shrewd man, Leahu, you've got your head screwed on right, that's for sure. But how did you manage to get yourself out of that backwater in Argeş and find yourself in the middle of Bucharest, in the police force, no less? Don't you have a house, land, family, back there?'

The guard scratched his head pensively:

'Yes, sir, you may wonder, as anyone may wonder, why a man would put down his plough and take up a job that no one in his family had even dreamed of . . . Of course! But you see, sir, there are many kinds of misfortune that can befall you, and no one runs away from home for no good reason. . . . If people like you, rich and educated, still have troubles to endure, what hope is there for us?'

'How did you end up joining the police?' Puiu insisted.

'Only because of my troubles, sir, how else?' Andrei Leahu continued with a barely suppressed bitterness. 'I was married, I had my own little house and patch of earth, like any decent fellow. And then the war came and it kept us all away from home, doing our duty, for as long as you gentlemen wanted. I was lucky and thank God I escaped with only one wound to my right leg, a trifle, you almost can't see it now. They made me a sergeant because I knew how to behave and had a little learning. Then, when they told us that they had made peace and we could go back home, I found my wife with a babe in arms. She'd gotten herself pregnant by a German who was in charge there in the village, then she had taken up with a Romanian and moved him into the house and now her belly was big again, like she had a pumpkin under her apron. . . . How can I tell you how my blood boiled at the sight of her? I started shouting: 'Woman, what have you done?' And still she quarreled with me, telling me that she had been told that I died in battle and what else could she have done, a poor woman, alone in the world, with no man to stand by her? She was lying, sir, and I was about to kill her! Then, seeing she had made a laughingstock of me, I gave everything up, the house and the land—because they were her dowry—left it all behind and ended up right here in Bucharest. Here I found my old lieutenant and I begged him not to leave me in the streets, as I had saved his life once in the war. It was he who encouraged me to take up a job in the police, as I was entitled to it, having been a sergeant. . . . So that's about it, sir!'

Puiu's attention became fixed on a single detail from the guard's story. He interrogated him with a hungry curiosity:

'And didn't you say anything to your wife when you found her like that?'

Andrei Leahu frowned at him and murmured gloomily:

'Of course I said a few things, sir! I said a lot of things and gave her a good beating, too. . . . But then I walked away so the devil wouldn't tempt me into a greater sin, because, God only knows, a man can do anything out of fury, and I didn't want to lose myself altogether and end up in prison because of a faithless woman!'

He gathered the cutlery and plates and took them to the kitchen without a word, downcast, as if the memory had exposed a deep wound. Puiu watched him until he was out of his sight.

'He could control himself when he was tested', he mused. 'And what a heavy blow he had suffered!'

He felt the wave of tranquillity that had enveloped him since his father's departure suddenly ebbing under the weight of his thoughts:

'A simple peasant had the courage to give up everything, to take on the unknown, build a new life, only to stop himself from taking the life of a treacherous woman!'

XIV

In the evening he refused to eat his food. The guard tried to encourage him:

'It would be a good thing, sir, if you tried to eat, even if you have no appetite! A grieving man shouldn't starve himself, it's a pity enough that his sorrows gnaw his heart, and besides . . .'

He couldn't finish his sentence. Incensed, Puiu exploded, as if the man had insulted him:

'Who asked for your advice, you imbecile? And how dare you bore me with your idiotic stories? Come on, get out, and I don't want to see your face until I summon you! Look now, who is giving me advice!'

Andrei Leahu, frightened, retreated out of the door with a bow.

Alone once more, Puiu paced around the room, fuming for a few moments longer, then crashed down on the bed, hoping that the stillness of his body would restore his serenity.

His distress bothered him all the more because he couldn't fathom its root. He kept reminding himself that he must be patient, like everyone kept telling him, even that fool of a guard. His situation was not as dire as it could have been. Instead of having being thrown into a prison cell, he found himself in a room at the sanatorium. All he had to do was wait for the denouement of this drama. He tried to imagine that he was really ill and was waiting for a serious operation that would leave him bedbound in this room, for a month or two. . . . Even though he was satisfied, in theory, with the logic of this argument, he was still ill at ease. Like the broken tip of an arrow, a fragment of a burning question burrowed in his mind: 'Why. . . ?' It didn't take long for the question to formulate itself, complete: 'Why did I kill her?' But he balked at this new question that nagged at him, demanding an answer that didn't exist. Finally, no longer able to bear it, he jumped to his feet and shouted loudly, as if to chase away a ghostly shadow:

'I don't know! I don't know! I don't know!'

His answer and the shrillness with which he had uttered it confounded him further. He looked towards the door, alarmed that the guard might have heard him and might consider him truly mad for talking aloud to himself. He commenced once again his nauseating march around the room, when the thought flew into his mind: 'I wonder how many thousands of times I will pace up and down like this before . . .' He couldn't finish his thought; finding himself by the window, an idea suddenly presented itself to him and he clung to it like a lifeline: 'If I couldn't control myself in the way that guard managed it, then that means that I was born with a criminal instinct!' The notion brought with it the natural conclusion that he couldn't be held accountable for his crime, as fate had poisoned his blood with an irresistible predisposition to violence. He must have carried this malady in his blood for many years yet, heroically, managed to suppress it. Yet in the end, in a moment of weakness, the unconquerable instinct took him by surprise, numbed his moral resistance, and compelled him to fulfill his destiny and become a murderer. In the same way that he had murdered Madeleine, he might have killed anyone, like *tante* Matilda for instance, if she had arrived that evening on time, or maybe even his own father. The instinct did not target a specific victim but would have been satisfied by any corpse, regardless of whose it was. And his accountability, in either case, would have been the same. A crime presupposes a question of will. But his crime. . . ? If things had been different, he might have been born with the instinct to commit suicide, rather than murder. In that case, instead of taking Madeleine's life he would have hurled himself out of the window or buried his head in the smouldering embers of the fireplace. . . .

He could see in a new light certain bizarre events from the past that he had never taken seriously and which had never troubled his conscience, consumed as he had been by the trivial trappings of daily life. Even his father's treatment of him seemed odd, although he hadn't realised it until now. For example, how he tried to shelter him from the company of violent friends, or how reluctant he was to allow him to hunt, only giving in after much persuasion and with a heavy heart. He remembered his father's words now, even though he had not taken them seriously at the time: 'It's not good for you to get accustomed to spilling the blood of any creature, even an animal.' And later, all of a sudden, he had said: 'I suppose, at the end of the day, it's better for you to satisfy your killing instinct by shooting rabbits and pheasants!' A little while before his wedding, not long after he had become engaged to Madeleine, he had got into a serious scuffle with his old friend Costel Plagino, over a woman, of course. He had slapped him, therefore they were required to fight in a duel. By the time the old man found out, the witnesses had already chosen the sword as the weapon for the duel and settled that it should take place the following day in a nearby field. Puiu was feeling relaxed about the fight: he was an accomplished swordsman and he had a special maneuver that no man had yet managed to block. He had joked with one of the witnesses that he would even give Costel a cut in his father's honour, so that he would learn a lesson not to be disrespectful to anyone. His father, however, despite knowing Puiu's reputation as redoubtable fencer (or, as he now contemplated, *because* of it), did everything in his power to prevent the duel, and in the end it didn't take place. In the evening, he told him in no uncertain terms: 'I don't want my son to be a killer, not even in a duel'. Puiu was now convinced that the old man knew of the terrible corruption of the blood that burdened his only son and tried to do all he could to save him from it.

'Poor father,' he thought, strangled by emotion. 'How he must have suffered because of me! And yet if only he had warned me, maybe I could have stopped myself! I could have tried to overcome the evil inside me!' He called Leahu to make his bed. The room was now dark, but he didn't turn on the light. He remembered how quickly he had fallen asleep the previous evening and he hoped it would be the same tonight, aching for the night to soothe him and clear away his thoughts. In fact, as he watched the guard making his bed, he thought how wonderful it would be if he could sleep for three months and only wake up once everything had been resolved in his absence. He slipped under the covers and ordered the man to turn off the electric light. He turned his face to the wall, just like yesterday. As he was going to sleep, he tried to summon from his memory other moments when the evil in his blood had surfaced. It was not long before countless incidents floated through the mind's mirror. The pleasure he felt, as a child, watching the cook cut the necks of chickens in the kitchen. How he would rush to press his hand on that headless body that writhed wildly, splattering blood in every direction. He felt again, disgusted, the burning of his bitter tears when the governess had held him back by force when he wanted to touch a decapitated hen. . . . And then his strange, irresistible instinct that overcame him at the peak of his passion to crush the woman in a mighty embrace or stifle her breath with one last kiss. Many women had called him a sadist, sometimes jokingly, sometimes not. Even with Madeleine, the first time he saw her, he had the impulse to clutch her to his chest until her life drained away. And to think that he had regarded this perversity as a sign of overpowering love. . . .

Sifting through his mind for memories that would support his theory, he turned in his bed, from one side to the other, without even noticing that he was now wide awake. Only at midnight he ordered himself: 'Now I must sleep!' But before oblivion could come, more and more memories swarmed him, whispering that his whole life had been a string of failed attempts to murder. . . . When he finally drifted off to sleep, he found himself in the salt mines at Târgul-Ocna, a place he had visited once, with friends, during a trip full of amusing escapades. Only now he was one of the convicts forced to work there, wearing a dirty, ragged striped uniform and cap, hacking away at an enormous block of salt, surrounded by monstrous figures who taunted him. The jibes of those criminal thugs wounded him like the stab of a knife. And then suddenly he was so enraged that he lifted the pickaxe above one of their heads, screaming: 'Quiet, quiet, quiet!' ready to strike him down. Then all of the felons jumped up and threw him to the ground, crushing him under their feet, while some of them loomed over his face with their mouths agape, champing their fangs like beasts, ready to devour him. He struggled under their weight but could not shake them off. He tried to close his eyes, to shut them out, but his eyelids seemed to have shrunk and remained peeled back, glued to the orbs that kept on swelling with dread. Cold sweat streamed down his cheeks and alarmed him more than the horror. . . .

XV

He didn't dare go back to sleep, but didn't rise out of bed until the guard entered in the morning with the day's newspapers. He got dressed and then went into the lobby so that they could clean his room and open the windows, hoping that the fresh air might sweep away all the ghosts that had crowded in that cell. He sat down at the guard's table and started leafing through the papers. He opened 'The Universe' and found himself stopping, unintentionally, at the penultimate page, the obituaries. His eyes skipped over the names and crosses until he found hers, modestly hiding at the bottom of the page: 'Mădălina. . . .'

'Why did they use her old name?' wondered Puiu, agitated once again.

He started to read: 'Puiu Faranga . . . Policarp Faranga . . .'

'They put my name first, even though I . . .' and he closed the newspaper immediately. He could imagine that it went on to talk about his 'endless sorrow' and other banalities that transformed this disaster into a drama for the elderly folk who entertained themselves by reading the obituaries.

'Poor Madeleine,' Puiu sighed once again. 'At least in death she can reclaim the name that was so dear to her!' He tried to divert himself by reading the news on the other pages, but his gaze kept sliding back to those black letters at the bottom of the page, trying to decipher them as if they were hieroglyphs. He read the day's events mechanically without comprehending the meaning of the words and after a time, he gave in and allowed himself to read the text in the bottom corner: 'The funeral will take place on Tuesday, 13th February, at 3 pm.'

'So, tomorrow!' Puiu thought. 'Tomorrow, it will all be over, all of it. . . .' He raised his eyes pensively. At that very moment, in the garden, a murder of crows swept down and settled on a branch laden with snow, like a wave of black thoughts. Puiu rose to his feet and turned his back to the window, distressed, as those birds had always disturbed him and now—just as he had been reading about Madeleine—they appeared like a sinister omen.

Andrei had finished cleaning his room. Puiu stepped back in, awaiting the doctor's visit, threw the open newspaper on the table and started wandering around the room. He had decided last night that he would explain to the doctor—after he had consulted with his father, of course—his theories about the cause of his crime and ask his opinion. Yet now he started thinking that it would be better to introduce the subject tomorrow. On the very day of her funeral, this revelation would lighten the burden of his guilt and serve as a pious offering to her memory. He remembered his foolishness yesterday when he had suspected the doctor of trying to take revenge on him because he had been secretly in love with Madeleine. It was a relief that he hadn't had the chance to share his suspicions with his father, who would have considered him ridiculous.

The doctor charged into the room, wearing the same sombre expression, and asked him curtly:

'What's new?'

'Nothing since yesterday', Puiu answered, trying to appear calm.

The doctor was only half listening to him, like the day before. He scanned the room, saw the newspaper on the table, picked it up and on seeing the obituary, read it with great concentration. When he finished, he turned to Puiu and, blinking slowly, with a tone that implied neither a question nor a confirmation, he said quietly:

'Mădălina?!'

Puiu was just about to explain yet before he could open his mouth to speak the doctor turned away from him and walked out of the room, followed by his entourage, muttering a strained and neutral 'Good bye.'

Her name, uttered by the doctor in that strange tone, echoed for a long while in Puiu's mind as he struggled to fathom its significance. Had he found it strange that in the obituary she was not referred to by the name she had been known in society, Madeleine? Then why had he not waited for an explanation, which he would have been only too happy to provide. . . ? Or was he mocking the pretensions of high society, where people change their names to some French affectation and only after death reclaim the name with which they have been christened, fearing that God might not recognise them in the afterlife? Or maybe the doctor knew exactly why it was Mădălina and not Madeleine and his mysterious observation was a hidden warning: 'I know everything, don't think you can hide the truth from me. . . .' If that was the case, the doctor had no reason to congratulate himself on his craftiness. The matter was well known, at least to anyone acquainted with Madeleine. It had not been a secret and the doctor might have heard about it any number of ways.

And yet the tone of his voice signified something. . . . All day long he was troubled by it. Little by little, the idea that the doctor was a strange man began to take root in his mind. He couldn't shake off the feeling that the doctor hated him. It shamed him to admit it, fearing that the thought was a sign of a malady, an insane paranoia. That's why he tried to blot it out of his mind and when he failed, he felt afraid. . . .

In the afternoon, the junior doctor came to visit him alone again to give him the news:

'I received a phone call from your father asking me to let you know that no-one will be able to visit you to-day, as everyone is busy making arrangements for the funeral. But tomorrow, after the service, they will stop by here. . . .'

'Thank you', Puiu whispered.

XVI

The following day found him in a great state of anxiety. He was anticipating the doctor saying something else that would make him lose control and demand explanations for those unfathomable allusions. The doctor, however, seemed even more sombre than usual. He was dressed in black. He looked at Puiu gloomily for a few moments without uttering a word.

'He must have realised that he behaved badly,' thought Puiu, satisfied.

But thinking about it later, he found the doctor's behaviour peculiar. Why had he stared at him in silence? Why was he wearing black on the very day of her funeral?

He soon forgot about the doctor as his mind became consumed with thoughts about the funeral. He was disappointed that no one had told him anything about the service. The closer it got to three o'clock, the slower the hands of the clock seemed to move. And then, when the time finally came for the funeral service to commence, Puiu knelt down by the window, his brow pressed to its frame, and began to pray fervently. The only prayer he knew was 'Our Father', but that seemed enough for now. He repeated it again and again, a hundred times, insatiably, with tears streaming from his eyes. In between sobs, he pleaded desperately:

'Forgive me, Madeleine, take pity on me!'

His knees, not used to such pious fervor, began to

grow numb. Sharp pain splintered through his joints. Nevertheless, he remained fixed in his place. The physical suffering felt like a relief from heartbreak.

That's how his father and Aunt Matilda found him, on their way back from the funeral. Darkness had descended and Puiu was still crouched by the window, shivering and cold, his lips bruised purple, chanting the same simple prayer. The old man gathered him in his arms and laid him down on the bed:

'What's all this, Puiu?' Faranga demanded, his eyes clouded with concern.

'I followed Madeleine into the grave that I sentenced her to', he whispered calmly, his face branded with grief.

The old man's bloodshot eyes filled with tears while Matilda, blowing her nose, muttered through hiccups:

'That was the end of poor Madeleine. . . . *Oh, mon Dieu, mon Dieu!*'

'*Soyez calme, Tilda!*' Faranga ordered her. 'Stay calm. It's over now! She, at least, is at rest, whereas the rest of us . . .'

'Poor, poor Puiu, how you have changed!' Matilda rejoined, swept up in a new wave of lamentations.

'Matilda! Enough!' Faranga cut her off firmly.

When Puiu asked them to tell him about the funeral, Matilda was in her element. In between smiles and tears she painted for him a picture embellished with the most trivial of details. She recited without hesitation the name of every distinguished person who had made their appearance to pay their last respects to Madeleine. She had been so beautiful, that darling girl, even in death, that no one could look at her without lamenting or weeping heartfelt tears for the loss of such a charming woman. She described the flowers, the procession of ten priests and a bishop, two government ministers, five diplomats, and all the finest dignitaries of Bucharest. Yesterday her body had been moved to the White Church, her favourite place of worship. Fifty thousand lei had been donated to the city's poor in her name. More than seventy carriages and cars had accompanied poor Madeleine to Belu Cemetery, where her body was laid to rest in the Faranga tomb, next to Puiu's mother. . . .

'You know, I saw your doctor in the church,' the old man intervened when Matilda's verbal torrent seemed to lose its momentum.

'Yes?' Puiu blanched. 'He was there?'

'*Ça l'honore!*' Matilda cut in. 'That does him honor! It means that he is truly a very sensitive man!'

And then, as Puiu was ruminating, frightened, on the significance of this news, she began describing with great enthusiasm the messages left with the flowers, the ladies' dresses, the expensive cars. . . . Her volubility numbed Puiu's shock at the news about the doctor and impelled him to ask if anyone had inquired about him. Matilda, encouraged by the question, burst out immediately:

'Anyone? Why, who didn't ask about you! Oh, *mon petit* Puiu, you have no idea how much everyone pities you and how faithful your friends have been in these tragic circumstances! It is only in misfortune that we find out who our real friends are! Well now, all, and I mean all of your friends bombarded me with questions and asked if they could come and see you. . . .'

Puiu listened to her emphatic reassurances with a wry smile. He realised that Matilda was exaggerating some formal gestures of politeness. He knew how things worked in their world and understood that his friends would try to distance themselves from any connection with him. Besides, his father had implied as much when he told him that he would have to live abroad for a few years, until the memory of his deed had faded . . . .

At last Matilda, running out of things to say, hurried to change the subject:

'But now, Puiu, let's talk about you! Poly tells me that you're settling in well here. *Et, vraiment, tu as raison . . .* You are absolutely right to do so.'

'Naturally', Puiu replied, sarcastically. 'One must get used to the direst of circumstances. . . .'

Faranga, who had been listening quietly up until that moment, intervened disapprovingly:

'What, my dear, you are not satisfied? Of course it's not Paradise here, but I would have thought that, under the circumstances, your situation is rather comfortable, extremely comfortable, if I may be so bold! If the doctor made the effort to show his face at the funeral, he must have realised who he is dealing with. . . .'

'Perhaps, . . .' Puiu murmured, with a slight shiver.

'And yet you seem more downhearted than yesterday', the old man persisted. 'Has anything happened? Is there anything you need?'

'Perhaps yesterday I didn't understand it all', Puiu mused. 'Shut away on his own for two days a man can learn more about himself than he might in twenty years living his normal life, in the outside world.'

Matilda, disturbed by his tone, cut in quickly, like a mother rushing to prevent a child from making a blunder:

'*Puiu, je te prie, il faut être sage,* please, you must be good, you understand?'

'*Oui, oui, tante Tilda*, of course I must be good!' Puiu smiled bitterly, with so much sadness in his voice that Faranga grew frightened.

'My dear boy', he demanded urgently, 'from now on you must concentrate on one thing only: waiting patiently. I and I alone will deal with the rest. Do you understand? If need be, I will take this matter to the king!'

'Bravo, Poly, that's . . . that's beautiful—it's heroic and superb!' Matilda exclaimed with admiration.

But Puiu bowed his head and after a moment, murmured:

'And my heart? And the painful battle I must fight every moment with my conscience, which accuses me and reproaches me with an abominable crime?'

'Without a doubt,' replied the old man, clearly moved yet struggling to maintain his composure. *'Mais c'est déjà autre chose!* That's something else entirely! For the time being, we must deal with the practicalities of the matter, and then . . .'

'Father, Father', Puiu suddenly cried, his eyes filling with tears, 'but I won't forget, I will live knowing that I'm her murderer!'

Faranga, disoriented, could only manage:

'Eh, eh, voyons! Come on!'

Matilda, however, interrupted indignantly:

'I don't want to hear those ugly words, Puiu, they appall me! Go on, you're only joking!'

'The seed of this crime was buried inside me always, it grew, it hunted me down, and finally conquered me!' Puiu concluded, exhausted.

'You are ill, my child!' Faranga soothed him, casting a look towards Matilda, who comprehended nothing. 'You should be in bed. . . . After such a terrible shock, it's no wonder . . . I will speak to the doctor. . . .'

'Please, Father, no, don't say anything more to him!' Puiu begged, transfigured by a sudden energy. 'I have very good reasons to demand this of you. Just leave him to do his duty in whatever way he deems to be honourable. I don't want to owe him anything.'

The guard appeared at the door with Puiu's dinner. He would have liked to turn him away, but his guests would not leave him until he had finished every last bite. Afterwards, they called the guard back in to make his bed, and only after they had tucked him in did they say their good-byes.

XVII

Faranga came by the sanatorium every morning, talking first to the doctor before going up to Puiu's room.

Yet the doctor wouldn't reveal anything.

'Patience and more patience! He must be kept under observation, with cases like this it is impossible to come to any conclusions immediately. At the moment I have ordered some tests: only after we know the results can we decide on a course of action. The patient is still very agitated. An emotional disturbance of this magnitude is likely to have powerful reverberations. Only hardened criminals can be immune to distress in such cases, because they have become desensitised.'

The doctor's explanations, although perfectly polite, were devoid of any warmth, either deliberately or due to a natural reserve.

'But you must have formed some kind of opinion?' insisted Faranga in a careful tone, masking the urgency of his appeal.

Doctor Ursu blushed a little and replied with the same politeness, drily:

'Your Excellency, forgive me. . . . I have given my opinion in accordance with my conscience as a man and a doctor. I pride myself on doing my job to the best of my ability—and I particularly want this to be true in your son's case. But I cannot forget that I am answerable to a tribunal that has placed on me the responsibility to ensure that justice is done. Under these circumstances, my own opinions about the case are irrelevant. However fond I may be of my theories, I cannot allow them to cloud my objective observations!'

Although the old man had nothing but admiration for men of honour, the doctor's words offended him a little. Nevertheless he thanked him, shook his hand powerfully, and commended him on how seriously he approached his duty. Privately, he began to feel afraid. His pride did not allow him to insist further or demand anything more from this young doctor, this perfect stranger. What he really needed from him was the kind of reassurance that could only be expected from a friend. Ursu must have ascertained by now the purpose of his daily visits, and if he had chosen to, he would have obliged him and told him what he wanted to hear, without further prompting. The fact that he insisted so vigorously on his duty and integrity could only be a bad omen.

Sensing that his plan was in danger of failing, Faranga decided to make discreet inquiries about Doctor Ursu. Everyone was full of praise: he was an exceptional doctor, very hardworking, well-read, knowledgeable, and, above all, a model of conscientiousness and integrity. He also found out that he was a country boy, his parents were peasants, very poor, and that all of his achievements were due to his hard work and perseverance; finally, that he was very young, only two or three years older than Puiu. With a man like that, it would be difficult to reach a compromise.

And yet Puiu had to be saved! One solution would have been to move him to a different sanatorium, where he would be treated by a doctor with whom Faranga could speak more frankly. But such a move would start tongues wagging, maybe even a scandal. Ursu himself, perhaps, might feel offended. Besides, he would need to have the move authorised from above. . . .

'If it comes to it, I will try that too!' Faranga told himself, resigned to wait a while longer. 'We will resort to such drastic measures later, if necessary.'

He did not, therefore, cease his daily visits to Doctor Ursu's office, and continued to ask him about every detail concerning Puiu. Incessantly, he turned over in his mind the possible motive for the crime, and became convinced that it was the result of some kind of subtle mental defect. In other words, the very thing he had dreaded, the irrevocable curse of a bloodline corrupted by centuries of inbreeding. . . . In this way, Puiu was only a random casualty and the real culprits were their ancestors who, in their stubbornness to preserve the purity of their kin, had multiplied in their offspring the seeds of perdition. It would be an appalling injustice if poor Puiu had to pay the price for a sin for which he could not—as any human heart would have to concede—be held responsible.

XVIII

Lately, Puiu wore a bitter smile as his permanent mask. On the day of Madeleine's funeral, he realised that he would only be able to find the comfort and tranquillity he needed to endure the troubles ahead by retreating into his very own soul. Although his father and Aunt Matilda were the two people he felt closest to, on that day it became clear to him that they were strangers to the torment of his heart. It dawned on him, at last, that every man is alone in his darkest hour. He became more and more convinced that he was stranded in a separate world, a world filled with confusion that had broken all ties—except in a practical sense—with the realm where others continued their lives. People, he reflected, spend their lives communicating through conventional signs and thus live under the illusion that they understand each other. In reality, we attribute our feelings to others and that which we call empathy is merely a mirror of our own souls. The only meaningful tie we have is with God, as only He, who has fashioned our consciousness, can truly understand us. Our greatest joys and sorrows we experience alone, cutting deep into our soul so that in those moments we might feel the sharpest sting of solitude. The revelation was all the more painful to him because it was the first time he had descended into the depths of his conscience. He had lived his whole life on the surface. His joys and disappointments had sprung from minor incidents in the world outside of himself.

His only goal in life had been the seduction of beautiful women and then, floating somewhere ahead of him like a hazy, distant target, the desire to follow in his father's footsteps by entering politics and even becoming a minister. His studies had been sufficient to earn him a diploma that he would never have to use. He needed some qualifications, however, for when his 'serious' life would start, at some point in the future. Ever since he had come of age, the old man had put at his disposal the fortune he had inherited from his mother, and this allowed him to live the high life, to satisfy his every whim and to enjoy an existence that was every young man's dream: parties, women, sport. . . . He wasn't interested in reading except as a cure for insomnia. Even the course he took at university bored him to tears. A life like his had no room for introspection or self-doubt. Up until then, the only thing guiding his conscience had been the malleable laws of fashionable society. Yet since this catastrophe had wreaked havoc in his life, he found himself face to face with the pith of his being.

For whole days he struggled to shake off the past and to see the present clearly. In this way he grew ashamed of the time before, when he had been entirely self-absorbed; when all that exercised his mind had been how to get out of a tight corner, through subterfuge, connections, any possible means; when his greatest pain had been the thought of having to renounce his life's pleasures for a while. Only a few days earlier, he had barely spared a thought for Madeleine, whose life he had extinguished, as she lay in the chapel waiting to be buried, and whenever the memory surfaced he would smother it again. There had been no heartfelt, deep repentance, as all of his thoughts had been consumed by fears of what fate would bring him.

It was on the day of the funeral that the fog started

to lift from his eyes. Kneeling beside the window, murmuring that prayer, he discovered his soul for the first time. Since then, her memory no longer frightened him, but illuminated his loneliness with her beauty. Whenever he closed his eyes, night or day, he saw Madeleine. She came into his room, sat down beside him, regarding him gently with her veiled, melancholy gaze, and that gaze dripped into his soul like a healing balm. She was silent just as she had been all her life: she never spoke to him. But he assailed her with questions, demanding answers and most of all begging her, amidst hot tears, to forgive him. She would smile again that wan smile and, in place of an answer, plant a kiss on his forehead with her cold lips. He always woke up, eyes moist with tears, after that kiss. And so Madeleine's memory became his only consolation.

XIX

On the seventh day Puiu was called again to Doctor Ursu's office. A feeling of discomfort had crept up on him without him even realising it. He couldn't suppress the feeling that the doctor hated him, and he instinctively responded with a sense of fear mixed with revulsion. He had become used to his daily visits and grown immune to his anodyne 'What's new?' and his piercing stare. Yet today he was anxiously anticipating another interrogation that would disquieten him as the doctor ransacked his past. His soul, he felt, needed only peace and silence.

The doctor, however, seemed brighter and more amiable than before. He spoke to him with greater deference, smiling from time to time. Only the expression in his eyes was the same, cold and suspicious.

'Well, sir', he began in a searching tone, gesturing for him to sit down on the usual chair, 'it seems that you have calmed down and we are ready now to talk properly.'

'Yes', mumbled Puiu, quiet and tense.

Ursu told him about the tests, about Faranga's visits, asked him how he was spending his time, what books he was reading, skipping from one topic to another without bothering to connect them, the words thickening into a fog designed to mask that searching gaze of his that sought to catch Puiu by surprise and force him to reveal himself. Puiu paid no attention to the stream of talk pouring out of the doctor's mouth, hypnotised by those eyes that he feared would pierce his soul. He was certain that the doctor knew everything: that there was nothing wrong with him, that he was completely sane and fully culpable of the crime he had committed, but that he was not yet giving the game away because he wanted to take pleasure in torturing him. He asked himself why, but became infuriated when he could not discover the answer.

'And now I'm afraid I'm going to have to ask you to clarify for me some details, perhaps a little intimate in their nature, but which I deem to be necessary in forming my view of this case. . . . Well, anyway!' said Ursu, rubbing his hands, and before articulating his thoughts, he moved to the desk and started rifling through some papers.

They were in Professor Demarat's office. It was brightly lit, full of books and medical instruments, with a couch that occupied most of the space and reminded Puiu of a camp bed and, in a corner by the window, a desk that seemed too small for the room. The walls were decorated with paintings and sketches, including the professor's portrait, and above the desk a photograph that had caught Puiu's eye since his first visit there: a slightly square, angular figure with sombre, piercing eyes.

'Yes, of course', he replied, shifting uncomfortably in his seat.

The doctor, now seated at the desk, bowed his head, gathering his thoughts, too embarrassed to continue. All of a sudden, he stood up and sat next to Puiu, and in a soft, entreating tone asked him:

'I saw that the obituary referred to your wife as Mădălina. . . ?'

Puiu flinched, suddenly possessed by an instinct to rise to his feet and refuse to answer.

He remembered the doctor's surprised exclamation

when he had read the obituary in the newspaper. And here it was again. . . . He replied irritably:

'It was her name. . . .'

'But I was under the impression that it was Madeleine, . . .' the doctor insisted. 'At least everyone knew her as Madeleine?'

No longer able to control himself, Puiu retorted curtly:

'How is my wife's name relevant to your medical inquiries?'

A flush of colour rose in the doctor's cheeks and his eyes glinted with malice, yet he replied calmly:

'Please allow me to decide what is and is not relevant. . . . Besides, I don't want you to think that the purpose of my questions is to bore you or to extract from you a disagreeable confession that would embarrass you or your family. Like I told you last time: in order to be able to determine your level of responsibility in a particular situation, I must have knowledge of every detail, no matter how insignificant it may seem, in case it might shed a light on that critical moment. . . . Of course, if you feel that my questions might touch upon some secrets that you'd rather not reveal, you don't have to answer and I will not insist.'

This shadow of suspicion aggravated Puiu even more. He found it unbearable that anyone, and particularly this doctor, would think there was a shameful secret in his or Madeleine's past. He answered immediately, with a forced, contemptuous smile:

'You're mistaken, and offend me, my esteemed doctor, if you suspect me of hiding anything from you! And it seems uncharitable to offend me when I find myself under your protection!'

'My apologies, my apologies!' Ursu earnestly protested. 'There is no question of suspicion here, or any desire to cause offence, and I have no wish at all to appear uncharitable. But when it comes to the doctor and the priest all superficial courtesy flies out of the window in order that confession may begin.'

'I wasn't trying to avoid the question!' Puiu replied, annoyed. 'I simply thought it peculiar that you should insist on certain details. . . . But if you really want to know, I'll gladly tell you everything! But be prepared for a long story, doctor. . . .'

'Just give me the gist of it!' said Ursu, contented.

He thought that he could detect an ironic suspicion in the doctor's eyes, and that made him more determined to go on. He began abruptly, nervously, choosing each word with great care:

'All of this started with one of my father's whims, just one of his whims. . . . You'll understand when I tell you and you'll agree with me! Because I was his only son, he was determined to ensure that the next generation would be more solidly built than I was. . . .' Puiu laughed, moving towards the chair. 'He, the old man I mean, had this funny theory, or maybe it had some basis in science, who knows. . . . Well, he said that our kin was doomed because of the inbreeding of so many generations and that it needed to be refreshed by new, young blood mixed with the earth. . . . Brrrr! And so, as I was the last of the Farangas, it was my duty to sacrifice myself for the sake of the family line and marry a peasant girl, whom he would choose for me in time. It did not seem much of a sacrifice to me. I thought that, given the status of my new wife, I would not be obliged to be faithful to her. Besides, there was something romantic and alluring about the plan: the idea of searching through all the villages far and wide to find a sweet peasant wife for a boyar. But these are just nonsensical ramblings, I only want to give you an idea.'

He suddenly stopped, wide-eyed, confused, his mind blank, then found again his train of thought and continued, with a smile:

'So, anyway! I came back from the war a sub lieutenant, like everyone else. I hadn't seen any action, of course, hadn't been anywhere near a battlefield. My father was very careful that I shouldn't become a hero. And then, as soon as I was out of uniform, he told me that he wanted to see me married straight away! Very well then! Let him find me a wife and I would be ready! But before he could . . .' Puiu made a gesture with his hand. 'I don't know how he was planning to find a girl to my liking. I never asked him. . . . Still, one Sunday, the old man decided that we would drive to my uncle's estate, in Argeş, Mănești, and spend around three days there. We were supposed to leave early so that we would get there at midday, but because my father had some unforeseen business to attend to, it was almost lunchtime before we left. We estimated we would arrive there at three.

On account of the bad roads and our worn tires—my father has always been mean when it comes to spending money on the car—we had several minor breakdowns, so that it was already five by the time we decided to stop in a village at least an hour away from Mănești. We were running out of petrol and starving, and then we chanced upon this inn, by the side of the road, a miserable place, just like the rest of the village. But what could we do? We stopped there to grab something to eat and for the chauffeur to refuel the car.

The innkeeper, a very shady character, insisted on preparing us a banquet and suggested that we should go and watch the village dance, saying that there would be many beautiful girls there and that the dance would take place just in the backyard of the inn. Because we didn't seem keen, the innkeeper insisted:

'You must see the Ciuleandra, if nothing else—they don't dance it anywhere like we do here. Our fiddlers are the best—it's a fine thing to see!"

'Yes, Suleandra', the doctor murmured, very quietly, listening with a cold gleam in his eyes.

'Have you heard of this strange dance before?' Puiu cut in immediately, surprised and delighted at the same time.

'Mmm. . . . yes', the doctor replied, unexpectedly startled, immediately regretting that the words had escaped his mouth.

There was a pause. Puiu smiled confusedly, waiting for the doctor to continue. Then, frustrated by his long silence, he resumed his story irritably:

'Well, yes. . . . Ciuleandra. . . . Anyway, the innkeeper led us to a verandah from which we could watch the dance as if from a box at the theatre. . . . At first, perhaps because I was hungry, I didn't think it was anything special. It was a village gathering like any other, the girls were so-so, the lads even less impressive. Besides, their dancing was fairly ordinary, spiritless. . . . And then the Ciuleandra began. Well, doctor, anyone who hasn't watched the Ciuleandra could never understand how intoxicating it is', Puiu exclaimed fervently, his eyes burning with ecstasy.

'It starts just like any other dance, very slow, very restrained. The dancers gather, form a circle, choose their partners, guided by lust, or maybe at random. Stirred by the heat of those bodies, the music quickens, grows wilder. The rhythm of the dance catches its frenzy. The dancers, gripping each other by the waist, build out of their bodies a wall that sways, tilts, writhes and trembles, in thrall to the music. As the fiddlers warm to their instruments, the melody twitches, spins loose, explodes into chaos. Sparks seem to fly as the lads scissor their legs, pounding the dust, leaping fearlessly through the air, shrieking with delight. And then, suddenly, everyone is swept up in a whirlwind, tearing the ground with sharp, swift kicks, flying! The living wall sways right, sways left, the fiddlers mercilessly pinch at their strings, the sound sharpened and coarsened by their savage cries, mirroring each other, then swallowed back into the tide of rhythm. And now the circle, swaying and coiling tighter like a formidable snake, begins to shrink, collapse onto itself until it becomes a heap of burning flesh that writhes, fixed in the centre, for a moment, only to loosen all of a sudden, mollified, tamed, exposing the raw, scorching joy branded on the dancers' faces. But the musicians, vexed by this lull, must have their revenge, and their tune screeches out harder, deeper, more insistent. The ring of dancers, daring themselves to defy and smother the music's spell, charge at it, feet crushing into dirt, and the tornado of flesh twists into itself again, tighter, more stubborn, clenching and loosening, until, finally, the bodies melt into each other like a fallen harvest. There, fixed in that spot, for a few minutes, for an eternity, possessed by the same maniacal rhythm, the bodies of men and women knead into each other, quivering, thrumming. Once in a while the simmering passion is pierced by long shrieks, erupting as if from ancient depths, or by the startled cry of a girl whose breasts were clenched too tightly. . . . And that's how it would go on until each dancer's soul melted into that all-encompassing flame of unbridled passion. But then, abruptly, like a chord sharply cut, the rhythm suddenly unravels and the young bodies splinter away with hoots of savage laughter and groans of pleasure satisfied, so that even the valleys seem to fill with trembling, as if the fury of human passion had unleashed the suppressed tremors of lust asleep in the earth. . . .'

Puiu came to a halt. His face was transfigured, his eyes ablaze, his cheeks glowing with an invisible mist of perspiration, his lips scorched by a fever. Only after a few moments, he remembered the doctor. Startled, he ran his hands through his hair, and carried on, straining to keep his emotions in check:

'I don't know what your impression is of this Ciuleandra, you said earlier that you were familiar with it, but I openly confess that even now, after all these years, I feel overwhelmed by a terrible passion when I recall it. Even my father, who is old enough not to be carried away, said to me, close to ecstasy, in French, because his enthusiasm can only find expression in French: *'C'est quelque chose comme une tarentelle collective ou comme une danse de guerre d'un clan sauvage!* It's something like a collective tarantella, or the war dance of a wild tribe!' In any case, to this day, I believe that only the Ciuleandra comes close to embodying the ecstasy that can erupt from dance, dance as a manifestation of absolute worship, resembling even those religious dances that culminate in mutilations or human sacrifices. . . . Anyway, I was spellbound and thrilled. I was waiting in a painful excitement for the dance to begin again, and I was afraid that it would not resume, because the dancers might be too exhausted. I couldn't stop asking the landlord if it was all over, but he reassured me, with a sly smile, that in that village the Ciuleandra would go on till the middle of the night, and that the dance would begin again as soon as the musicians had rested a little. I was as anxious as if I were about to sit an exam I had not prepared for. And then, suddenly, the musicians began tuning their instruments! The Ciuleandra was about to start again. I could barely wait. I whispered to my father, still in French: 'I want to try this dance, *Papa*, what do you say?' Smiling, he answered me: '*Vas-y!* Go ahead!' Before he could answer, I was already there, amongst them. I latched onto the circle at random. I have always believed in the power of fate. I feel certain that fate, or even chance, with its whims, is the engine behind all significant events in history, indeed, I would say that it is the force behind everything that has ever happened in the universe. Well, then, this mysterious master of our destinies gifted me, to my right, an extraordinary dancing companion, an incredibly delicate dark-haired girl who seemed to have climbed out of a portrait by Grigorescu, with a pair of blue eyes, moist, ablaze, that gazed at me so strangely that they ravished the very depths of my soul. She was quite tall, shapely, bare-headed, with two plaits flowing down her back. I put my arm around her waist. Her flesh was as hard as stone. She clenched her left arm round my neck. I could feel the roughness of her hand, burning into my skin and teasing me like a caress. I turned my head towards her.

Her white blouse, embroidered with flowers, covered her small breasts, their contours straining against the cheap fabric. She looked back at me and laughed mockingly, with her wondrous, contemptuous mouth. Then she immediately turned her head away, perhaps embarrassed to be looking at me or ashamed that others might see us. But the dance had begun. I didn't know the steps but there was no need. The rhythm of the music and the movements of the others swept me away like a wave. Sometimes the girl's body touched me by accident and I would pull it tighter against me. When my arm clenched harder round her waist, she submitted, with a little frown to signal that she did not approve. This aroused me even more. That a little peasant like this should resist me when I was renowned as the most eligible bachelor in the finest salons of Bucharest? In the heat of the dance her body was pressed against me so tightly that I could feel her breathing. I was dizzy, as much from the whirl of the Ciuleandra as from the greedy desire that the maiden had awoken within me. I reached towards her and kissed the corner of her mouth. Surprised and unable to defend herself in any other way, she sank her teeth into my cheek, like an angry cat, and then gave a sharp, satisfied yelp. One of the lads laughed, roughly: 'Don't give up, boyar!' I laughed foolishly, as did the girl, blushing and exhausted. And then I kissed her once more after a few moments, when our bodies were once again thrown together in the dance, and she couldn't retaliate this time, only frowned crossly. Later, when the Ciuleandra had ended and everyone began drifting away, I realised I was still holding her hand.

'What's your name, pretty girl?'

'Mădălina Crainicu', she murmured, embarrassed, peering at me under her eyelashes.

'Mădălina what?'

'Mădălina Crainicu', she whispered quickly, then pulled her hand out of my grasp and ran as fast as she could towards a tree to join a group of giggling girls. I stood there, fixed to the spot, watching her, mesmerised. Mesmerised by the dance and mesmerised by the girl. When I came to my senses, I walked back to the verandah and announced to my father in a tone of passionate determination: '*Papa*, I have found what you were looking for!'

The old man received my declaration with a certain coolness. It wasn't enough that I liked her—he had to approve of her, too. Still, he made enquiries about her at the inn. We found out that Mădălina was the daughter of a poor widow, an honest, hardworking woman.

'But the daughter, what is she like?' my father inquired.

The innkeeper bowed respectfully:

'What can I say, sir? I mean, you can see that she's only

a child, about thirteen or fourteen. You wonder how it came about that she joined in the dance. She must have felt like it, she's not a shy one and she dances well. . . . But surely that doesn't mean. . . ?'

But my father persisted:

'How did her father die?'

'In the war, sir, struck down by a German bullet at Predeal!'

Then my father asked if he could take a closer look at her. Obligingly, the innkeeper shouted right away:

'Come on, everyone, see if you can find Mădălina Crainicu, the boyars want to see her!'

And then to my father:

'If you would be so kind as to take her into service, it would be a blessing to her family, as her mother can barely cope with all those children. . . .'

Mădălina was pushed, reluctantly, onto the steps of the verandah, where the innkeeper took her by the hand, gently chiding her:

'Don't be silly, girl, the boyars just want to have a look at you!'

My father, examining her carefully, asked her a few questions, some of which she answered, while for others the innkeeper was left to fill in the details.

By that time, all the dancers had gathered around to find out what the boyars wanted with Mădălina. In order to break up the crowd, even though he would have liked to interrogate her further, the old man let her go, so that she could return home. He grew quiet, and when the innkeeper's interjections came to an end, he declared gravely:

'She's a nice girl, no doubt, but we must think about it carefully.'

'Father, you must understand, she's the one I want!'

I noticed that he did not seem aggrieved by my ardour,

just as he had not taken a dislike to the girl. A quarter of an hour later we left, travelling without any further troubles to Măneşti. We were there for two days and my father did not utter another word about Mădălina. Yet I could sense that she was on his mind and that he was hatching a plan. We left on the third day and, on the way back, we stopped again at Vărzari.

The innkeeper guided us to Mădălina's mother's house, recounting to us, in detail, the story of the girl's father, who had been the strongest man in the village, a good, capable man mourned by everyone who knew him: 'It would have been better if we had lost ten of the others, if only he had come back to us!'

Mădălina's mother virtually collapsed with astonishment when she saw us entering her yard. When she managed to compose herself, she invited us in. It was a squalid, filthy house like you would only see in the countryside. Mădălina attempted to tidy up as best she could, embarrassed that the guests should see the way they lived. We sat down. Solemnly, gravely, without any further ado, my father made his intentions clear: he wanted to take Mădălina away from that place so that she would eventually marry me. The widow was overcome with shock. The innkeeper, too, seemed taken aback, like this was the last thing he had expected. Indeed, he looked at us askance, suspiciously, probably wondering whether we were some kind of swindlers that wandered around the countryside luring women and then disposing of them in some kind of sinister fashion.

The old man, however, began to elaborate: Mădălina would be adopted by my Aunt Matilda, she would be given the best education and then later, at the appropriate time, would become my wife. He hoped that the girl would grow to love me. In addition to adopting Mădălina, he would bestow a dowry of fifty thousand lei on the widow's youngest daughter. . . . The woman couldn't believe a word of it, she merely grinned idiotically, wiping her mouth with the corner of a handkerchief while periodically shouting at two sprogs that were fighting behind the oven. Anyway, to cut a long story short, after an hour of bargaining, the matter was settled. My father and the woman shook hands while Mădălina, who had been flitting in and out of the room, now curled up into a ball by the door, weeping, babbling, petrified, with growing horror: 'Don't give me away, Mummy! Mummy, don't give me away!' So that there could be no doubt about the legitimacy of our arrangement, we all walked to the town hall, where my father repeated again his declaration that Aunt Matilda would adopt Mădălina and his promise that the widow's youngest daughter should receive a dowry, placing in her hands, in front of the mayor, ten thousand lei, with the rest to be sent over once the legal adoption of Mădălina had been finalised. . . . And then Mădălina was dressed in her best clothes, the clothes in which she had danced the Ciuleandra, and we put her in the car and drove back to Bucharest. . . .

'Yes!' Doctor Ursu said suddenly, his voice harsh and strange.

Puiu stopped, confused, perturbed by the doctor's tone.

'I only interrupted you because you seem to have grown tired!' the doctor added immediately, noticing the effect of his interjection.

Puiu's face brightened. The doctor's attention flattered him.

He hadn't felt tired, but now he felt vanquished by a kind of torpor. Still, wanting to repay kindness with kindness and feeling obliged to finish his account of

Madeleine's story so that the doctor could be fully informed, Puiu began again with a grateful smile:

'Thank you, doctor, you are very kind, but I'm fine. . . .
So, as I was saying, we arrived in Bucharest and went
straight to Aunt Matilda's house. Father told her that she
should treat Mădălina like a daughter and, most importantly, to make sure that I couldn't get at her in case. . . .
Well, my poor aunt was stunned to be presented in this
way with an adopted daughter, found in some backwater, but she was relieved to hear that my father would be
solely responsible for her dowry. He reassured Matilda,
who was by nature quite miserly, that her fortune was
safe, that she could still leave it in her will to whatever
distant relatives she wanted, if she thought them more
worthy than this adorable girl.

During the following days, there were endless serious discussions between my father and
Aunt Matilda about Mădălina's future. The first thing
that needed to be settled was, of course, her education.
A formidable German woman was swiftly employed to
give her enough polish that she would be ready to be sent
abroad. In a month, Mădălina had changed beyond recognition. She had become an enchanting young lady, her
charm heightened by her gaucheness. My aunt changed
her name to Madeleine from the second day after she
arrived. She said it came to her more naturally, as my
aunt had a passion bordering on mania for anything
French and believed that every well-bred lady should
speak French with a Parisian accent. The girl did not, of
course, object to the changing of her name, just as she
did not object to anything else. She did confess to me,
however, a few days later, that she preferred Mădălina,
as it had a sweeter ring to it—something that I agreed
with, as did my father. But we had to indulge Aunt Matilda, especially as she had grown so fond of Madeleine

and made it her mission to mould her into the most distinguished young woman, claiming that Madeleine possessed the nature of a real lady.

A month later, my aunt and my father put the girl on a train and accompanied her to Switzerland, to a finishing school in Zurich—the best in Europe, as my father would always tell everyone—where for a year she would follow a special programme and be tutored in French and German. Aunt Tilda went over there to visit her five times to check on her progress, and each time she returned, she was full of praise: '*C'est une petite merveille, Poly!* The girl is a little marvel!'

As for me, whenever I misbehaved, she threatened me that I wouldn't be allowed to have Madeleine, as I did not deserve a girl like her. Even though the original plan was that she should stay only a year in Zurich and then spend a year in Paris, then another one in London, my father decided to keep her in Zurich for another year to make sure that she was ready. As he was paying for everything, including Matilda's visits to Switzerland, no one objected to his demand, even though my aunt protested that it would have been better for her to spend a year in France, as she felt it was the only country that could truly civilise one's soul. . . .

Meanwhile, I was to leave for Paris to do my doctorate there, to please my father. I only saw her once in Zurich, chaperoned by my aunt, who had travelled with me to get me settled in France. That's when I found out that Aunt Matilda had not been exaggerating in her reports. Madeleine was, indeed, a marvel. It is amazing how quickly women can adapt to new circumstances! Anyone would have thought that she had been a princess from birth, her appearance was so refined, her gestures and deportment so effortless. Naturally, we spoke only in French, and I was ashamed to admit that she spoke infinitely better than me, even though I had been chattering in Voltaire's tongue ever since I started to talk. Later, when I lived in Paris, even though they brought her there too the following year, I was only allowed to see her twice, once with Aunt Matilda and the other time with my father. Finally, when I returned home with the diploma in my pocket, she was sent to England, for the final stage of the programme. The following autumn she returned back home. Enchanted and delighted, Aunt Matilda introduced her into high society straight away, and just as she had predicted, Madeleine mesmerised the whole of Bucharest. I began to realise that my aunt could very easily make good on her threat: at any moment, at least ten suitors, all of them superior to me, would be ready to fall at Madeleine's feet.

Of course, there was a vast difference between the Mădălina from a few years ago, dancing the Ciuleandra, and the new Madeleine, a difference not only in her demeanour but also an alteration of her soul. Mădălina had been joyful, exuberant, almost wild, whereas Madeleine was gentle, discreet, and melancholy—and her melancholy veiled her eyes, her smile, her voice in mystery and, people said, made her all the more alluring. That winter, my father reminded me that I was twenty-seven years old and Madeleine was eighteen, therefore it was time. . . .

I was happy. I can't think of any other conversation with my father that has ever brought me so much joy. During those four years, I had done everything I wanted, had countless affairs, but Madeleine had remained enshrined in my heart like a holy icon. I adored her all the more since our separation had imbued her with a kind of mystery. And so, after a formal engagement and extensive preparations, the ceremony took place after Easter, four years ago. . . .'

Puiu was quiet for a few moments, deep in thought, the memories transporting him to another world. He looked at Doctor Ursu, who was watching him in silence, smiled, and continued:

'You see, it's no great secret.... How could we ever hide this from the world and why would we even try? Anybody who was interested could learn of our story. On the other hand, of course, there was no need for us to announce it in the papers! It was a private matter, concerning only us. I had no reason to be ashamed of Madeleine just as she had no reason to be ashamed of Mădălina!'

The doctor, strangely animated, persisted:

'This is all very well, but I still don't understand why in the obituary she is named Mădălina!'

'Well, how am I supposed to know, doctor?' Puiu said, disappointed that his story was not enough to satisfy the doctor. 'I imagine that my father did it to honour her memory. Because at home, we still called her sometimes, affectionately, Mădălina, and she loved it. And the name seemed to suit her better in those days, tamed and sweet as she was, than it ever did before....'

Ursu remained silent, a little perturbed. He seemed to be trying to formulate another question or perhaps trying to process everything he had heard. Puiu's face reddened, but his eyes shone bright and clear. His whole face seemed to glow with the flames of those reveries and the doctor, noticing this, stood up suddenly and said sharply:

'Thank you.... I'm sure you're tired....'

'No, no', Puiu protested with heartfelt sincerity. 'You have helped me a lot, doctor, you have no idea! At first, I have to admit, your question irritated me, you must forgive me. I hadn't realised that by forcing me to remember I would regain those happy moments, that I would relive them and rediscover my little Mădălina and fall in love with her again. It is the greatest gift you could offer me. Thank you, thank you!'

Seized by emotion, he rushed towards Doctor Ursu, grabbed his hand, and shook it vigorously. After escorting him to his room and leaving him in the care of the guard, the doctor washed his hands, as if afraid of infection.

XX

From then on, Puiu began to look forward to the doctor's visits, almost regarding him as an old, benevolent friend. He always smiled at him, full of trust, even though the doctor never responded in kind and in fact appeared even gloomier than before. But Puiu ignored all these signs. He told himself that he was only imagining the doctor's dourness, just like he had imagined that there had been some kind of history between him and Madeleine. Absorbed in his own inner turmoils and battles, he reasoned that it would be fatal to exaggerate the importance of every gesture, to suspect everyone of being an enemy. . . . He now accepted that these thoughts had all been the product of his feverish mind, of a heightened, morbid sensitivity. . . .

One day, when Puiu was in much better spirits, old Policarp Faranga entered his room more agitated than usual. He asked the guard to go out into the corridor so that he could talk to his son in private. Puiu couldn't help smiling indulgently at his father's mysterious, indignant manner:

'Has something serious happened, Father?'

'Yes, Puiu, very serious indeed!' Faranga said, rising to his feet, as if ready for combat. 'This doctor is a scoundrel! *C'est une canaille!* You understand? *Une canaille!*'

'You're exaggerating, Father!'

'Not at all, not at all!' the old man objected, annoyed. 'I have made up my mind. I must get you out of here at any cost, I'll move you to another sanatorium, I'll place you in the care of a good man! *Voilà!*'

'But why now, when I have started to feel so much better?' Puiu persisted calmly, beseechingly.

'You would feel much better in a place where the doctors were real human beings, where they were on your side rather than enemies!' Faranga burst out, then checked himself and lowered his voice. 'Besides, I've already talked about this at length with Tilda. She entirely agrees with me: we have to get you out of here, you have to escape from the clutches of this odious doctor! I brought you here because I assumed that you would be treated by Demarat, a man in whom I have complete trust. I never imagined that. . . .'

He was growing more and more heated as he talked. He paused, pulled at his beard—always the sign that his fury had reached boiling point—then walked a few steps closer to Puiu and said in a calmer tone:

'Last night, at the club, I was talking to Professor Dordea. He asked me how you were getting on and that's how we got talking about Doctor Ursu. Dordea knows him well, he was his student. Well, can you guess what Dordea told me? "An admirable student, an excellent doctor, in fact", he said, "but an altogether impossible man!" You understand? What do I care about his professional qualities if, on all accounts, he is a terrible person? Dordea remembered how at university he never missed an opportunity to have a dig at the "toffs", meaning, of course, just about anyone in respectable society. His outbursts were so well known that Dordea himself asked him once how he, an educated man, could bring himself to voice such barbarous opinions? But all that he could get out of him was that the "toffs" had broken his heart, and other such ravings. So, you see: the simple fact that you're a "toff" means that this savage will seek to destroy you with his insane hatred!'

'Perhaps Dordea was exaggerating or misunderstood him', Puiu murmured, unfazed.

'Not at all!' the old man stubbornly persisted. 'Dordea is not one to speak lightly and he doesn't listen to gossip. The only reason he saw fit to tell me these things was to warn me so that I should be careful and act before it is too late. Obviously, since he is also a doctor, he couldn't accuse him of anything directly. But his words are corroborated by the various opinions of Matilda's friends, some of whom have been patients here, in the sanatorium, who knew Doctor Ursu personally or had other friends under his care whom they visited, and therefore heard about him from them. Well, everyone agrees that he is nothing but a coarse peasant. Mrs Ferentaru—you know her—was truly inspired when she said that she never saw a man whose name suited him better, this "Ursu" truly is as savage as a "bear"!'

Nevertheless, Puiu's faith in Doctor Ursu could not be shaken, and he refused to be moved to another sanatorium.

'Very well, then, Puiu', his father chided him, 'but don't forget that your life depends on this man! On his reports! It isn't wise to allow a man who is a sworn enemy of your class to have control over your future.'

Finally, realising that his entreaties were falling on deaf ears, the old man confessed that despite Puiu's insistence that he should not intervene, he, Policarp Faranga, had visited Ursu daily and that despite his subtle allusions, he had never been able to draw out of him a single reassuring word or any hint that he might be on their side.

'I can barely bring myself to tell you that once he was almost rude to me', he concluded miserably. 'I didn't say anything to him at the time because I didn't want him to turn against you. It was bad enough that he dared to be impolite to me, a man older than him and in a position that should demand some respect!'

Still unconvinced, Puiu answered dejectedly:

'What greater harm could he do to me than that which I have inflicted on myself? That he should decide that I am fit to stand trial? So what? Would that be a greater catastrophe than Madeleine's death?'

'But it would mean *your* death, Puiu!' the old man cried. 'It would mean a second blow for me too! One is enough. Another must be prevented at any cost! Not even poor Mădălina would have wished for such retribution!'

His eyes filled with tears. He turned towards the window, took out his handkerchief, and, pretending to blow his nose, fought back his tears before Puiu could see them and become upset by the sight of his father crying.

'I didn't bring you here', he continued, 'so that we would be back where we started. I'm begging you to put an end to this sentimental attitude, which is entirely at odds with the circumstances.'

Puiu began to protest, offended:

'Really, father, you seem to think that these cheap legal tricks actually matter! As if, were I to be released, I could ever give a damn about the outside world! To become part of it again, you're asking me to lie, to pretend to be mad. . . . Well, I can't do it, father, not for any price! I don't want to deceive, to burden my conscience even further, with lies, just to escape the punishment I deserve for my crime. I can't! And even if I were treacherous enough to try to pretend, I just wouldn't know how to. So, in the end, I will just stay here, just as I would stay anywhere else, content to accept whatever fate awaits me.'

'It's true, you're right', old Faranga whispered. 'You wait here day after day, tormented by thoughts and I bring you these. . . . *C'est fini!* I'm done!'

And he left the room, looking as miserable as his son. Each one inwardly complained that the other did not understand him.

'I must concentrate on the present, for the future will take care of itself!' Puiu told himself, resigned, but feeling somewhat proud that he had not given in to his father.

' *Il faut agir, Tilda, mais sans plus compter sur lui!*' old Faranga complained to Matilda back at home. 'We have to act, but we cannot count on him!'

And Matilda vehemently agreed: 'That's right, dear Poly! *Il faut le sauver malgré lui.* We have to save him in spite of himself.'

XXI

Because Puiu could not bear to look at the newspapers, he asked the guard to read them out to him, and in this way they became more entertaining. Andrei Leahu read each word out syllable by syllable, and this was exactly what Puiu enjoyed most about the experience.

He wasn't in any hurry; quite the opposite, the slowness with which the guard read out the stories filled the time and sped it along. And as the news did not really interest him, he focused instead on the man's intonation, contemplating how much he resembled a conscientious schoolboy, enjoying his commentary on the stories, a commentary mostly comprised of wild speculations rather than rational inferences. Leahu was especially excited when he came across something about Argeş, his county, in the papers; and once, when he noticed the name of his village in a list of places visited by an uncommonly energetic minister, he kept going back to that page all day, sighing pensively, full of concern:

'So, he went to our village too! I wonder what brought him there, what could have happened?'

Puiu, who noticed how much pleasure it gave him to talk about this village, kept asking him to tell him everything he remembered about his home. Timid and uncertain, Leahu always started by telling him about the boyars he knew, what they looked like and how they behaved, about the disagreements between various people one particular year, about the time some folk from Sze-

kler came down. . . . Yet he always finished with anec-
dotes about his fellow peasants, of which he seemed to
have an endless supply.

After the old man left, in order to chase away his dark
thoughts, he went to the guard's anteroom and lay down
on his bed, as usual, and they began their daily chat. But
after a while, just as Leahu was getting into a story about
a girl who fell pregnant and then went to Pitești to get
rid of the baby and find a job in service to get away from
the village where everyone would point at her and never
let her forget, Puiu suddenly interrupted him, sitting up
and staring at him as if through a haze:

'But in your village, how do they dance the Ciuleandra, Andrei?'

'Well, sir', began the guard, slightly taken aback by the
interruption but pleased by the question, 'the Suleandra
is a difficult dance and you need a lot of dancers as well
as good musicians who know the tune well. Very difficult indeed!'

Puiu meant to tell him to carry on with the story about
the girl, but he heard himself asking:

'Have you ever danced the Ciuleandra?'

'Sure I have, sir!' Andrei boasted. 'God knows how
many boots I've ruined dancing the Suleandra! It drives
a man crazy, that dance!'

'Excellent dance!' Puiu burst out, unable to contain
his excitement. 'I also danced the Ciuleandra, only once,
at Vărzari. . . . It was a wonderful thing! That's where I
chose my wife, dancing the Ciuleandra. You know, the
one I strangled, you understand. . . ? Yes, the Ciuleandra . . . my wife!'

He heard himself saying things he did not want to say
and yet the strange, unfamiliar voice ran on until even
the guard started looking at him askance. Still, Leahu
agreed, politely:

'Well, around our parts, all the lads find their wives at the Suleandra. They get close to the girl they like and hold her tight and dance and burn until they lose their minds. . . . It's that dance, sir, it does that to you!'

Puiu listened to the guard, distracted, struggling to remember the Ciuleandra music, and the fact that he couldn't sorely tormented him. It crossed his mind that he should try out the steps of the dance so that the music would come back to him. He realised that the thought was insane and tried to swat it away, afraid that the guard would think that he had lost his mind. At the same time he couldn't stop himself asking:

'Listen, Andrei, could you whistle the Ciuleandra for me?'

'No, forgive me, sir', Leahu answered, alarmed and embarrassed by the request. 'I've never learned to whistle, God knows I've never had an ear for music.'

'Shame', Puiu murmured, standing up suddenly, on an impulse. 'I would have liked to see you dance to it, but I can't remember the melody, otherwise I'd happily whistle it for you!'

'I still wouldn't dance to it, sir!' said the guard, laughing awkwardly and trying to hide his unease. 'It wouldn't look too good either, because the Suleandra is a sprightly dance and I'm a bit long in the tooth for it! It's a young people's dance, sir, for young people as strong as beasts, and I squandered all the strength I had in the war and through other misfortunes, it's a wonder I'm still alive. . . .'

'Oh, you're a fool, Leahu!' Puiu retorted with barely suppressed fury. 'You boast that you know all about it but you don't know anything!'

'Really, sir, don't upset yourself!' Andrei pleaded, trying to pacify him. 'It's getting dark and the ladies and gentlemen in the other rooms are really unwell, not like you, and they go to bed early and get disturbed by noise. . . . Anyway, if anyone were to see me skipping around in here, there would be hell to pay if the doctor heard about it!'

With a painful effort, Puiu prevented himself from asking again. He could clearly see how odd his obsession with the Ciuleandra must seem and realised that he could no longer control what came out of his mouth. In order to quash the temptation that constantly reared its head in his soul, he ordered Leahu to make his bed so that he could go to sleep. He had got used to going to sleep with his door open. Now he asked him to close it. Defying his will, his subconscious mind was still struggling to recall that wretched tune.

He undressed, got into bed and, trying to smother the urge that rose up inside him uncontrollably, shut his eyes and pulled the covers over his head. Fragments of the melody started to crowd his mind like a swarm of angry bees. A note would rise from his memory and buzz in his ear, then dwindle again, leaving behind it only a more urgent need to remember. Under the covers, he started to whistle furtively each new snippet of the melody as it passed through his mind.

He soon gave up. It was nothing like the real thing. And then, frustrated, he jumped out of bed and, standing on tiptoe, started to reconstruct the steps of the dance, quietly, so that the guard would not hear him and conclude he had gone mad. He struggled for a quarter of an hour and still he could not piece together the Ciuleandra. But after he tucked himself under the covers, his body drenched in sweat, he felt oddly at peace as he told himself: 'I will remember it. . . . I won't give up!'

XXII

After a disturbed night crowded with strange dreams, Puiu woke up feeling tranquil and filled with quiet determination.

He washed and groomed himself more meticulously than on the previous days. He stared at himself in the mirror for a long time and decided he looked dignified. His pale, gaunt face, the lustre of his skin as it stretched over his cheekbones, slackening at the corners of the mouth, his haunted, sunken eyes, all revealed a new man, completely different from the perfumed, pampered dandy of old. He told himself that these were the marks of his recent anguish and felt pleased to see evidence that he had suffered so much, believing that his torments had brought him closer to Madeleine.

He placed the mirror upright on the table so that, whenever he passed, he would catch a glimpse and admire himself, passing the time until the doctor's arrival, which he awaited more keenly than ever. Finally, Doctor Ursu arrived with his entourage and asked him the usual question:

'What's new, Mr Faranga?' He appraised him for a moment, threw a glance around the room, and then made for the door. But Puiu's urgent plea stopped him in his tracks:

'Doctor, please, I have an important confession to make!'

Ursu stared at him searchingly.

'Please! I'm listening!'

'Oh no!' Puiu protested, defensively. 'It's something rather delicate which I'd like to discuss with you in private. . . . It's very important to me, doctor!'

The doctor stared at him for another moment and conceded:

'Very well, I'll call for you once I have finished my visits.'

Puiu was possessed by an overwhelming excitement. Agitated, he paced around the room, muttering broken phrases as if preparing a speech, passing from the guard's anteroom, where Leahu had laid out the newspaper ready for their daily ritual, back to his own room. . . . A couple of times he sent Leahu to see if the doctor had finished his visits. The answers annoyed him because they were always the same: 'almost' . . . When the doctor finally called him, his body suddenly stiffened and he walked solemnly out of the room, followed by the guard.

'Well, I'm listening!' the doctor said to Puiu as he entered his office. He was still standing, taking off his white coat.

In his presence, Puiu felt overwhelmed by emotion, his voice strangled by sorrow:

'Doctor, I have discovered why I murdered Madeleine. . . .'

Ursu flinched. He threw the white coat on a chair and drew closer to him.

'It wasn't easy, of course', replied Puiu, smiling with satisfaction at the doctor's disbelief. 'I'm not surprised you don't believe me. And yet it's true. It has been a struggle, my soul has been shaken to its foundations, yet I have discovered the truth. Yes, it has been a tremendous struggle!'

The doctor could not conceal his bewilderment. He was clearly hesitating, unsure what to believe. He asked him to sit down and tell him the whole story. And Puiu, after a long introduction embellished with all sorts of minor details, explained how he had come to realise that he had been cursed with a hereditary criminality and how this had been simmering under the surface all of his life until the moment when it flared up uncontrollably and he killed Madeleine. As he was telling the story, Puiu grew paler, his hands started to tremble, yet on his face flickered the smile of a martyr.

'Everything is perfectly clear to me now', he added, his eyes shining with elation. 'You can't imagine, no, no one can imagine how terrible I felt when I came to this realisation! It is no small matter to realise that all of your life you had been harbouring criminal instincts and that each day has been a minefield of potential violent outbursts which you have managed to smother only through your will and through your breeding, and that for years you have lived with this immense burden lurking in the depths of your soul! Today I wonder how I even managed to live like this, why no one opened my eyes to what I was!'

Ursu managed to regain his composure. After a moment's silence, he inquired calmly:

'But this still doesn't answer the question why you chose to kill your wife rather than anyone else?'

'You don't give up, do you, doctor?' Puiu suddenly snapped, irritated. 'I killed her because she happened to be there! Don't you understand? If the maid had been in the room instead of her, or even you, a complete stranger, I would have strangled either of you just the same!'

Agitated, he clenched his hands in front of him, convulsively, as if gripping onto an invisible throat. The doctor watched him and retorted sternly:

'Is that how you strangled her?'

'Probably', Puiu quickly replied. And then, suddenly

confused, he carried on in a lowered voice: 'I can't remember exactly. . . . You know, during those moments, the only thing that you are conscious of, the only thing that seems real is that instinct, numbing and blinding everything else!' After a brief silence he continued, his voice reduced almost to a whisper: 'And besides, when I am furious, I am transfigured, I take on the look of a savage. Somebody told me once, jokingly—I don't remember who but I remember the words exactly—that I resemble a caveman when I'm angry!'

'Mmm . . . yes, . . .' the doctor murmured, lost in thought.

'The only important thing you should take from all this, doctor', Puiu resumed, flooded by a new wave of excitement, 'is that the murder was the product of my inherent criminal instinct, you understand? When I first arrived here I was confused, I couldn't comprehend how I could have committed such an odious act. Well, finally, today, after three weeks of ceaseless soul-searching, everything is clear. The real truth is that I'm mad! I have come to this realisation all by myself, doctor! I didn't submit to a moment's madness, as my poor father would like to believe, but my mind is undeniably, irredeemably diseased! Unfortunately, this is the reality, doctor!'

A short, dry laugh escaped from his throat and echoed through the room like the rattle of broken glass. The doctor shivered, as if chilled by a gust of cold wind.

XXIII

'Listen, Andrei, do you believe that I'm ill? Or do you think that I'm not? Tell me the truth!' Puiu asked the guard that same evening, with a queer laugh, as the man was busy changing his bed.

'What kind of illness are we talking about, sir?' the guard laughed, in return. 'A gentleman's illness? Whenever a gentleman gets himself into trouble, he's quick to blame it on some illness, and everything gets settled fast enough!'

Like everyone else in the sanatorium, Leahu knew that the gentleman was feigning madness in order to escape prison. That's why he paid little attention to his odd behaviour, thinking it had been contrived to deceive him and turn him into a witness to his unbalanced mental state. Apart from his scheming, he reckoned that the gentleman was a good sort, easy to talk to and warm-hearted. Deep down, despite his loyalty to the police, he admired his craftiness: why, just because he had made a mistake and killed a woman (and what woman doesn't, after all, deserve to be murdered, he often wondered, after the disgrace his wife had brought him), should a good man have to give up his life? He knew of other cases from his time in the army, where someone had tried to wriggle out of going into battle or dodge some kind of punishment by pretending to be mad. But there they wouldn't get the same treatment as in a place such as this, there they would be wrapped in cold wet sheets and scolded until they lost their appetite for play-acting.

Puiu, who had first broached the topic, initially intended to tell him about his conversation with the doctor. But now he changed his mind and asked the guard to tell him about other such cases he had known from his work as a policeman. He listened contentedly for a while, but then stopped him abruptly:

'Wait, wait, Andrei, let me tell you what happened to me. You can't know what really happened just from the newspapers, because no one, except for me, truly knows the facts. But I want to tell you, I want you to know!'

'You mean . . . what happened to the lady?' asked the guard.

'Yes. . . . I feel I can tell you, we're like brothers now after spending three weeks together side by side, like comrades in the war, bunking together. . . .'

But he lost his train of thought and stopped, confused. Before the words could come to him, he heard himself asking another question:

'Listen, Leahu, you fought in the war, didn't you, you were on the front? So tell me, how many men did you kill in battle?'

The guard laughed:

'Well, sir, no one keeps count in the war, because no one kills willingly, without orders from above. But still, I swear to God, I don't think I actually killed anyone there. Sure, I used to shoot and I must say I was a good shot at that, but I don't think that even one man died by my hand!'

Dissatisfied, Puiu insisted:

'But were you never part of an attack?'

'I was, sir, certainly I was, we all charged at them with our bayonets, but even so, God help me, sir, I don't think . . . When I was in battle, I would hit them with the handle, which seemed easier to me, somehow. Certainly, I slapped a few of them about that way, but I was too God-fearing to kill them, because even in war there is no need to kill the enemy if you can beat them hard enough that they don't come after you.'

Puiu looked deflated and spoke contemptuously:

'So that's why you didn't kill your wife, even after she disgraced you!'

'Well, I'd say I was lucky I didn't, sir, otherwise I'd be rotting in prison on account of a wretched woman!' Leahu quietly replied, with a bow.

'. . . while I strangled my wife even though she was entirely blameless!' Puiu concluded triumphantly, a cruel gleam filling his eyes.

As the guard's only answer was a shrug, Puiu continued:

'No, I'd go so far as to say that my wife was an angel, my boy! But I was cursed by God with a criminal instinct and fate brought her to me in that evil hour, the poor soul. . . . You see, all of my life I had been battling it, that murderous urge, and I might have killed countless times if I hadn't summoned the strength to control it! If *I* had been sent to the front, I would have killed a thousand Germans at least!'

'Well, the Germans didn't let themselves be killed as easy as all that!' Leahu gravely observed.

'Whether they did or they didn't, it doesn't matter!' Puiu grew furious. 'I would have shot them all, no doubt about it! And if I had killed them, then I wouldn't have killed my wife, can't you see? That's the truth of the matter: I was born to kill someone. . . . Now that I've taken a life, I have fulfilled my destiny and I don't need to kill anyone ever again, it is finished! This entire mess with my wife is my father's fault, because he asked them not to send me to the front!'

'Each man's sin is his own', the guard, full of humility, murmured, 'but God forgives every man.'

'Forgives, forgives, of course he forgives', Puiu whispered to himself. 'How can he not forgive those who know how to pray to him. . . . But what about the others? Because prayers . . . a prayer should be constant, forever unchanged, the same prayer over and over again, and no other. . . .'

He suddenly became aware of the senseless words pouring out of him and stopped, wiped his brow, smoothed back his hair, and then said, in a dejected tone:

'Let's go to bed, Andrei, it's late. . . . My sin weighs down my soul, it is too much to bear. You know, I feel it here, sometimes, as heavy as a millstone. . . .'

'Take heart, sir, for God is good. . . .' The guard tried to comfort him.

'Even if God is good and even if He forgives me, I cannot escape my sin, its burden, this crushing burden from which I cannot find relief! Better to say, God save me, Andrei!'

'God save you!'

'Good night!'

XXIV

The following day he asked if he could go for a walk in the gardens of the sanatorium. The guard bundled him into the winter coat they had brought to him from home. The sting of the cold, early March morning invigorated him. The snow had almost entirely melted, only here and there white patches spotted the black earth. The stiff branches of trees shivered as the spirit of the spring had breathed into them wave after wave of new life. The smell of damp leaves, like the vital scent of the earth, stirred a new strength and resolve in his soul. He walked brightly and swiftly on the wet paths, and the sound of the thawing gravel crunching under his boots filled him with pleasure.

'Spring is coming, Andrei!' Puiu murmured, breathing in deeply.

'Yes, sir, it's coming', mumbled the guard, his voice tinged with nostalgia. 'Back where I'm from, the people will be cleaning their ploughs. . . .'

They reached the railings separating them from the street. An empty tram passed by; they could see the conductor in the middle carriage counting the money while sucking intently on a pencil. A car appeared from the opposite direction and then vanished again into the distance, with a long hoot. Puiu thought that it was exactly the same sound as the one that the horn of his own car made. Two children, on the pavement, had stopped to peer between the railings, as if staring into an enchanted fairytale garden; when they spotted Puiu and his guard they ran away immediately, frightened, thinking they had disturbed some apparitions. Puiu walked to the same place by the railings where the boys had stood and looked out into the now-deserted street. Across the road, a fashionable house, with iron gates and a white facade with three windows, wore a springtime smile. Puiu gazed at it longingly; it reminded him of the house in Iași where they had stayed before the war. On the prim white wall he could see two small plaques, one with the name of an insurance company, and underneath it a blue one with the house number painted in white.

As he had nothing better to do, he strained his eyes to read it and then startled, agitated by some bad news.

'What's that number, Andrei? I can't quite make it out', he asked the guard quietly.

'Thirteen!' Leahu proudly announced, after a silence of several seconds.

'Thirteen?' echoed Puiu. It was just as he thought, but, with a cold shiver stirring his heart, he tried to persuade himself that he had made a mistake. He had never been superstitious. In the past, when others had expressed their aversion to that fatal number, he had pretended to loathe it as well. In fact, to him it was just like any other number, as it wasn't in his nature to worry about such things. Yet now no amount of reason could dispel the vague and unsettling feeling that started enveloping his soul, like a veil that thickened with each passing moment. After three weeks of torturous solitude, why did he have to see a house with the number thirteen the first time he ventured outside his room? It was a question impossible to answer, yet it drilled into his brain, like a secret ache. He continued his walk around the garden, trying to shake off the oppressive burden. But he was sick of walking. The air seemed humid and suffocating.

The viscid mud stuck to his boots. Everywhere he looked he was struck only by ugliness and filth: the dry, broken branches, scraps of paper, rotting fruit—the traces of winter, exposed by the melting snow like sores on the cheek of a sick man.

'That's enough, Andrei!' Puiu said, irritated.

He went back inside, bored and shivering from the cold. As he entered, he noticed for the first time above the door of his room—the room where he had spent so many days—a plaque with the number 76 written on it.

'It's a good thing that it's not the number 13, at least', he pondered.

Yet while he was undressing, the number floated again through his mind, and after a while he heard himself saying:

'Seventy six, so a seven and a six, which add up to thirteen again.'

He decided not to waste his time dwelling on these childish coincidences. Surely it was only his feverish brain that sought an ill omen in everything he encountered. Only fools place so much significance on such meaningless trifles, he decided, while he, an educated man, must rise above them and swat his fears away. Nevertheless, despite his resolve to dismiss all such thoughts from his mind, an irrepressible impulse burrowed into his consciousness, searching for other such coincidences. He remembered the obituary in the paper and for the first time registered the date of Madeleine's funeral, the exact shape of the letters and numbers rising clear before his eyes: 'Tuesday, 13th February . . .' Just as he was about to riposte that it would have been more significant if she had died on the thirteenth, he suddenly remembered that his first meeting with her at Vărzari, the day of the Ciuleandra, had also taken place on a fateful date: Sunday, 31st July. In that instant he remembered that somebody had once told him that the cursed number was all the more dangerous in its mirror image. While the evil effects of the number 13 could be annihilated, the number written backwards would unleash a catastrophe impossible to avert through any human effort.

'That's just how it was for poor Mădălina,' Puiu said to himself, starting to search through his memory for all the dates that might have led to his doom.

His own birthday was 31st March. When he recalled the individual numbers of the year his mother died, they added up to 13, and he had graduated from college in 1913. . . .

All of the coincidences he discovered riled him so much that in order to drive them away he went to the anteroom so that he could distract himself by conversing with the guard. Leahu had gone to have his dinner, however. Just as Puiu was starting to get annoyed at this, he remembered that even the number plate on his car, 1331, had a 13 in it and a 13 backwards.

'And yet I never even had the tiniest of accidents', he mumbled to himself gleefully as he returned to his room. 'Which means that the fatal number brings me luck!'

But after a while he decided that the two numbers must have cancelled each other out. And if it was a question of luck, that luck could only have belonged to his father, because he was the one who had passed down to him his old number plate. Again, he tried to swat away these thoughts, deciding that these were merely the ravings of a hysterical man, driven to distraction by solitude. On reflection, he decided that being in the sanatorium had actually been worse than prison, because the doctor who was meant to care for him never took his condition seriously and didn't even bother to pretend, acting more like a prison warden, constantly scrutinising him. He hadn't even conducted any proper tests aside from the ones routinely given in the hospital. Instead of trying to get to the root of the problem, the doctor merely interrogated him constantly about every detail of that dreadful night, betraying the fact that the murder and the circumstances surrounding it interested him more than his patient. Everything in the doctor's behaviour displayed a hidden animosity, just as his father had argued a day earlier. He had been perpetually quiet, surly, almost deliberately trying to exasperate him. His first instincts about the doctor had been right, even though he initially tried to smother them out of fear that he was being paranoid. But now there was no longer room for doubt. His father had been perfectly right. This doctor, who tyrannised him instead of helping him, was solely to blame for the fact that he could no longer control his nerves, that he was terrifying himself with imaginary number patterns.

'Even my wedding to Madeleine took place on an unlucky day', he suddenly interrupted his train of thought, as if all the time that he had been trying to chase away the irrational fear, it had been hiding behind a corner, magnifying and swelling so that it could erupt again, even more insistent. 'It was on 31st March and we got engaged on 13th February. And then exactly four years after our engagement, on the same day, her funeral! How could all these mean nothing. . . ? Poor Madeleine! From our first meeting to our last hour, everything had been cursed by those fatal magic numbers! It is clear to me now, we were both cursed to endure an awful destiny. Perhaps she was even born on the 13th. . . ? It's true, I don't remember her birthday. Not even the year she was born. But I can try to calculate it: four years of marriage, four years abroad, and she was fourteen when we met. It's no good, I can't remember the day. . . .' He spent the whole day tormenting himself by turning numbers in his head and concocting various ominous interpretations, and when his father came to visit him as usual in the afternoon, he questioned him impatiently:

'Father, what was Madeleine's birthday?'

'The last day of the last month of the year!' Faranga answered promptly, with a forgiving smile. 'I hope that I've made myself clear?'

'The last . . . so you mean 31st December!' Puiu murmured, growing pale. 'Thirteen backwards . . . just like me!'

Old Faranga was quiet for a few seconds, confused, and then said authoritatively:

'Puiu, dear, if you start on things like that you're going to make me upset! I don't know what's happened to you, my darling!'

'I don't know either, Father!' Puiu replied dejectedly. 'All day I've been thinking about this number, all day! It's like a nail has been hammered into my head and I can't pluck it out!'

'Nonsense, Puiu!' the old man caressed him, the blood draining out of his cheeks. 'You need to be patient, just for a couple more days! I've put everything in place for your move to another sanatorium and you will be out of here in a couple of days! And then . . .'

Puiu's empty eyes scanned his father's face and he burst out in desperation:

'Yes, Father, yes! Take me away from here, please! I can't do this anymore! I feel like I'm losing myself here, I'm losing my mind, Father! The doctor! The doctor, Father! He won't let me be, believe me, it's true! He is my enemy! I tried to befriend him, I bit my tongue, I humiliated myself, all for nothing. He wants to destroy me, Father! Every night I dream of him piercing my brain with long needles, mercilessly, each and every night. . . .'

He was sobbing now, his head pressed against his father's chest, and the old man, horribly shaken, patted him on the back, murmuring:

'*Voyons, Puiu, voyons* . . . Now, now, my son. . . .'

XXV

Eventually, Puiu calmed down once again, feeling his soul purged by his tears. The prospect of the move to a different sanatorium filled him with hope. He was waiting for that moment, imagining it held the promise of redemption. The old man had said it would be a few days; he didn't care if it was a week, as long as he knew he would soon escape the doctor. That same evening, he announced the news joyfully to the guard:

'Eh, Leahu, we'll both get out of here soon!'

'God help you, sir, because you've been suffering here for more than a month', the guard answered quietly. 'It has been no bother for me, I've lived better here than I do at home, I've been well fed and barely had any work to do. But you, on the other hand . . .'

'We're leaving, Andrei, I don't care where we are going as long as we get away from here!' Puiu added, his flushed face shining with happiness, gazing at the guard with so much affection that the man grew embarrassed.

Puiu's suffering had won him a place in Andrei's heart. He understood that the conscience of a man who had taken the life of another would naturally be burdened, especially if the person he had murdered was the wife with whom he had lived in harmony for many years, yet it seemed pointless to him that the gentleman should still be tormenting himself, now that it was too late to do anything about it. To him, the only appropriate response would have been silence, that is to say a submission to the blow that fate had dealt him.

As usual, when he was in a lively mood, Puiu wanted to chat. This time, however, he felt like gossiping about the sanatorium and Doctor Ursu.

'He's a very surly man', the guard dared to suggest, after it became clear that the gentleman did not hold a high opinion of the doctor.

'I bet he doesn't even treat the staff very well,' Puiu encouraged him. 'You can tell that man is a bad sort from the moment you meet him. I still remember, for instance, that first morning I saw him, the way he came in looking miserable, staring at me with eyes full of hatred, completely silent. . . .'

In fact, Andrei Leahu couldn't stand Doctor Ursu, because he had never shown him any respect, his tone always arch and insulting. Every morning he had found an opportunity to criticise him about something, in front of others. He felt humiliated at the fact that he was treated like a servant, a nobody, even though he had been sent there by the superintendent to do an important job. But he never shared his feelings with anyone, not even Puiu, even though he could tell straight away that the gentleman did not get on well with the doctor either. He told himself that it was better to keep his mouth shut: gentlemen squabble and then make their peace again, but he didn't want any trouble to come his way. Besides, for all the indignities and insults, he still liked working there. He didn't even have to touch his wages, as he was well looked after, and the tips from old Faranga were even greater than his pay, as every time that gentleman came to visit—and he never stayed away longer than three days—he never forgot to give him a little present, always whispering the same short instruction: 'Look after him, boy, look after him well!' This was why he now regretted revealing his feelings to Puiu, and began once again to evade his questions.

'Everyone always wonders why the doctor is so harsh, seeing as he's no better than any of us', he ventured, thinking himself safe by hiding behind the opinions of others.

'Precisely!' Puiu agreed. 'I knew he was born a peasant.'

'That's right, sir,' Leahu continued. 'The chef here tells me that he used to go to school with him. He knows him pretty well, they used to work together in a big hospital in Brâncovenesc before they settled here. And he said that the doctor's family is as poor as dirt and that they live around our parts, in Argeş.'

'In Argeş? What do you mean, in Argeş?' Puiu leapt up, animated.

'Yes, sir,' the guard insisted. 'He's from Argeş, from a village I've passed through many a time, a place called Vărzari.'

'What Vărzari?' Puiu replied, astounded.

'Well, I only know of one Vărzari in Argeş—' the guard answered, confused by the gentleman's agitation, 'it's a place just off the main road between Piteşti and Râmnic!'

'Seriously? From Vărzari?' Puiu repeated, pensively. 'How strange.'

Andrei peered at the gentleman and, seeing him so disturbed, wondered whether he had said the wrong thing. He would have liked to fix his error but he didn't know how. He couldn't feel guilty, though, because he knew he hadn't told any lies or done anything wrong. Puiu would have liked to talk more with the guard to pass the time, but he could no longer stand it, as all of his thoughts now whirled around the new piece of information he had just received. So Doctor Ursu was from the same village as

Mădălina! That was why he seemed so interested, that was why he wanted to know so much about her! And yet, when he had told him the story of how they met, he acted like he had never heard of Vărzari! He only gave himself away when he corrected him on the pronunciation of Ciuleandra, calling it 'Suleandra', like the locals, with that sweeter Moldovan lilt.

'How strange', Puiu murmured again, retreating back to his room. But then, at the end of the day, none of it really mattered anymore.

XXVI

'I'd like you to come to see me today!' said Doctor Ursu in a mellifluous tone that grated on Puiu even more than his usual harsh manner.

He managed to control himself impeccably. He had decided, after considering at length how he should best use the new information he had received, to act as if nothing was amiss, not to mention anything, as ultimately he was going to be moved somewhere else and he would never have to set eyes again on Ursu.

He had been called to see him late in the day, probably after the doctor had finished his visits. Yet today he was waiting calmly, free from the agitation of the previous days.

The doctor received him amiably, shaking his hand with a smile that stretched into a grin:

'Well, Mr Faranga, I venture to say that very soon your trials and tribulations will be over!'

Puiu, who assumed that the doctor had found out about his father's intervention, shrugged and remained silent.

'What, you're not even a little pleased?' continued the doctor in the same honeyed tone.

'It's all the same to me now', Puiu grumbled.

Ursu stared at his patient searchingly for a moment as if wanting to confirm a theory he had already formed, then burst into a peal of laughter, like the screeching of a saw:

'But that's just empty talk, my dear sir! No one, in your situation, can receive this kind of news without a jolt of emotion!'

Because Puiu remained apathetic, the doctor, instead of divulging how Puiu's torment would end, continued confidentially:

'You know, Mr Faranga, that I haven't been able to get this Ciuleandra of yours out of my head, I think I am getting as obsessed with it as you were!'

Filled with contempt, Puiu scrutinised him for a second before answering with the same calm:

'Doctor, you mention the Ciuleandra.... Very well. I confess that I was and still am obsessed with it, I feel I've been touched by a fatal curse. But sir, you cannot honestly tell me that it was the first time you'd heard of it?'

'What?' Ursu flinched in surprise.

'Are you not originally from the village where they dance the Ciuleandra?' Puiu persisted.

'So?'

'And are you not in fact from Vărzari, the village where I once danced the Ciuleandra and where I met Mădălina?'

'So?' the doctor drily repeated.

'So ... so ...' Puiu mimicked him with steely self-control. 'So when I was telling you about your village, about the dance that you knew....'

He stopped abruptly, suddenly struck dumb. He remembered how he had resolved not to make any suppositions about the doctor. His face regained its serenity and his gaze was vaguely tinged with irony.

Ursu did not seem offended by the insinuations, but appeared irritated by the fact that Puiu's tirade had come to a sudden halt. His cheeks were flushed and his nostrils trembled. He waited for a few moments for him to continue.

Puiu sunk deeper into silence.

'You think that I should have repaid your confessions by revealing all my intimate secrets?'

The doctor turned to him with a sharp glint in his eyes, his voice as hard as a rain of boulders rolling down a mountain. 'You forget that it was my right and my duty to extract these confessions from you! So let us not exchange roles now!'

He regained control of himself and calmed down immediately. His body relaxed, the searching look returned to his eyes and his lips stretched into a forced smile:

'You've provoked me and managed to make me lose my cool . . . and naturally I should always maintain my self-control, shouldn't I?'

'Probably', Puiu answered coldly.

'But you have made an accusation that was almost an insult to me as a doctor', Ursu carried on calmly. 'You seem to imagine that there was an ulterior motive behind my questions about certain delicate matters from your past, you don't understand that I was merely doing my duty. . . . Yes, yes, I know what you were implying! Well, you have to understand that you are completely wrong, Mr Faranga! And you have to understand it particularly because I have done everything I can to explain to you why I am obliged to persist with these questions. The best proof of that is the fact that I have gathered important information from these confessions to support my verdict on your case.'

Puiu remained silent. After a brief pause, the doctor continued:

'For instance, the Ciuleandra! It annoyed you how much I insisted that you tell me all about it. Well, I was convinced that the Ciuleandra played a part in your crime! In the way you described it to me and from what I remember of it. . . .'

'Tell me, doctor, please, have you ever danced it?' Puiu couldn't resist asking him, with a greed that destroyed all his resolve. The doctor glared at him for a second, trying to ascertain if it was a serious question or whether he was being mocked. Puiu's eyes flashed like fireflies in the evening gloom.

'Yes, of course I have danced it!' said the doctor slowly and deliberately. 'And I liked it!'

'It's a mesmerising dance, doctor, it's incredible!' Puiu insisted, his eyes aflame. 'It's a fearful whirlwind that stays with you till the day you die!'

A tremor coursed through his body and he was suddenly seized by an impulse to leap up from the chair, to run out of the room. Frowning, he suppressed it and continued with an almost furious enthusiasm, unable to control his trembling knees:

'And it is exactly your village that is the nest of the Ciuleandra, Doctor! I heard that there is nowhere else in the world that they dance it as wonderfully as they do there!'

He leapt to his feet, unable to bear sitting still any longer, hesitated for a moment, then added confidentially:

'Now I must leave, doctor, right now! But before I go, please, because you must know, it must be in your blood, please tell me how the melody of the Ciuleandra begins? I struggle and struggle to remember it but I can't, I can't remember it at all. . . . And it is such a distinctive tune! Unfortunately, I have no ear for music and perhaps that's why it hasn't stayed in my mind and I cannot recall it. You can't imagine what pleasure it would give me! Mădălina played it on the piano for me sometimes, she was incredibly musical, and I would dance to it, well, I mean, just skip around. . . .'

He felt like showing him how he used to skip to the

music. He stopped, tired and embarrassed, because he had been talking very quickly, as if someone was chasing him, his voice pleading and his face shining with desperate hope. The doctor tried to detain him, asking:

'I am not musical, so I'm not much use to you. But, if you like, I can see if I can find the melody for you. I'm not sure, but perhaps I can find it. . . .'

'Oh, thank you so much, Doctor, with all my heart I am grateful to you, believe me!' Puiu cried, swept up in a wave of enthusiasm. 'Through this promise, you have proved to me that you have a good soul! They told me that you are fiery and vindictive and I must confess I believed them, but now I know in the depths of my heart that it was all calumny! Anyway, I must leave now, excuse me! Maybe I'll remember the Ciuleandra even before you find it for me, who knows? Good fortune comes to us when we least expect it. . . .'

He ran out of the room, followed by the guard, who barely managed to keep up with him.

XXVII

'Andrei, lock the door!' Puiu whispered as he entered the anteroom. 'Come on, lock it, lock it, I want to try something!'

The guard locked the door, confused, looking at the boyar who carried on jubilantly and mysteriously:

'The doctor has given me an idea, Andrei! Not intentionally, of course, because he's a cunning one! He refused to whistle the Ciuleandra for me, he pretended not to know it. . . . As if he wouldn't know it! He thinks that without him I'm not going to remember it! He told me: "I'll see if I can get it for you", thinking that he's pulled the wool over my eyes! As if the Ciuleandra was the Charleston, and you could find it on music sheets, to be played in a salon! Well, I'm going to show him that he can't make a fool of me and I will dance the Ciuleandra in front of him tomorrow, he won't believe his eyes! But you've got to help me. Andrei, are you listening? Don't pretend you don't know it, you're from Argeş, for God's sake, you were born with the Ciuleandra in your blood!'

He rubbed his hands, elated, while the guard kept mumbling and trying to pacify him:

'Wait, sir, we'll remember it, don't rush it. . . .'

'Good, that's right, Andrei!' Puiu nodded approvingly. 'We mustn't rush! Let's take it slowly and plan it properly! Only those who plan carefully manage to succeed in the world, like this doctor of ours!'

He went to his room to get changed. As he was getting dressed, he whistled and hummed the melodies of different dances, some slow, some fast, correcting himself impatiently after each one: 'That's not it, young man! It's wrong, all wrong, forget it!' At one point, his efforts seemed ludicrous to him and he chastised himself out loud:

'Puiu, you're an idiot! What's got into you about this Ciuleandra? Nonsense! Pure nonsense! Stop it right now! Is this really the time to be obsessing about this Ciuleandra of yours?'

Next door, the guard had sat himself quietly on his bed, listening to the gentleman's tormented mumblings and pitying him. He was genuinely sorry that he couldn't remember the Ciuleandra tune, otherwise he would have whistled it for him and perhaps then he would be content.

'To hell with the Ciuleandra!' Puiu announced, suddenly appearing in the doorway dressed in a brown dressing gown; his face looked fatigued, yet gentle and smiling.

Joyful, Leahu rose to his feet:

'Absolutely right, sir. Shall I go and see if your dinner is ready?'

'Yes, go, go, Andrei!' Puiu agreed, soothingly. 'I'm suddenly starving, I could eat you in one gulp!'

The guard laughed happily and blessed him as he went out of the door.

'That's right! Now I've got rid of you!' murmured Puiu, breathing easily again. 'Why would I want to make a spectacle out of myself and look crazy in front of a simple man like that? But I can't stand for the doctor to mock me for not being able to remember the Ciuleandra. . . . No, that will never happen! I haven't completely lost my mind!'

He withdrew to his room and, whistling vaguely,

started the first few steps of the dance, with great concentration, gently swinging his hips, his arms stretched out as if he were holding the waist of an invisible dance partner. After a while, he chided himself softly:

'Not like that, sir!'

He tried another tune, with a different rhythm, but the same steps. Still unsatisfied, he altered the melody again. Then all of a sudden, inflamed by a revelation, he told himself:

'I am beginning in the wrong place, that's the trouble! It's not the melody that's important, but the steps, the dance itself, the music comes second, to shore up the rhythm! It's obvious that the melody needs to mould itself around the dance, not the other way around! That's why I never got it right and why I could never feel satisfied!'

He started again immediately. He swayed his arms and legs, twisted his body while humming a random tune. Tirelessly persisting, he kept telling himself encouragingly:

'That's right! You see? That wretched tune, those very steps!'

The rhythm was getting livelier and livelier. He stepped forward, bent backwards, his feet sizzling, as if he was stepping on burning coals.

His forehead sprouted hot beads of sweat that poured in rivulets down his temples, through his eyebrows, over his cheeks. From time to time, an anguished cry sprang up from the vaults of his lungs and then his visage lit up in ecstasy.

He continued like this for another quarter of an hour until, exhausted, he collapsed onto the bed, where he remained motionless, with his eyes closed, breathing heavily. The same look of enchantment remained imprinted on his face and a sense of triumph rose in his heart as his dry lips mumbled:

'At last, I've got it!'

When the guard returned with his dinner, Puiu, a little more rested yet still prostate on the bed, greeted him hoarsely, yet with evident pride:

'Andrei, I've done it!'

'What have you done, sir?' asked Leahu.

'The Ciuleandra, boy!' Puiu explained. 'I've got it! Fantastic! Aha, you all thought I'd never remember it, but I have! I'll show it to you, but not right now, some other time. . . .'

He was hungry. He hurriedly swallowed a few bites of food and then fell asleep, waking up only after midday when old Faranga arrived. The old man was glad to find him in bed, resting. He didn't allow him to get up.

'Stay and rest, Puiu, get your strength up! Besides, I'm not staying for long. I only came to tell you that everything has been sorted out: the Board has granted permission for you to be moved to the Crucea Albă sanatorium, under the care of Professor Dordea, you know, the one who spoke to me about Doctor Ursu. The move will take place on 13th March, the day after tomorrow, which should give us enough time to get everything settled.'

A shiver ran through Puiu's body as he suddenly started to mumble:

'Thirteen . . . thirteen again. . . .'

Faranga became annoyed:

'*Mais tu es maniaque, mon enfant!* My child, you have gone mad! You hold onto these superstitions that no one takes seriously except for wet nurses and sick old hags.'

'Father, please *je te prie, je te prie beaucoup*,' Puiu pleaded,' I don't want to move on the 13th! I'd rather not move at all!'

Not wishing to unsettle him, the old man relented:

'Alright, if it means so much to you, we'll move you on

the 14th! Seeing as you have been given permission to arrive there from the 13th onwards, one more day won't make a difference.'

But Puiu shook his head sorrowfully:

'No, father, it does matter, because the 13th will be the one-month anniversary of Madeleine's funeral. . . .'

'So. . . ?' Faranga replied, a little confused. '*Mais ce sont des enfantillages grotesques!* This is such ridiculous childishness! You have no idea how much I regret the fact that I listened to you in the first place rather than pulling you out of here straight away, as soon as I noticed your doctor's strange manner! If I had done so, you would have been out of here a long time ago and maybe your soul might have healed!'

'The healing of the soul', Puiu smiled wryly. 'Yes . . . healing. . . .'

In the evening he paced around his room for a long time, unsettled, occasionally entering the anteroom as the guard watched him in silence, until at last he announced:

'I have given it a lot of thought, Andrei, a lot of thought: I'm not going to move away from here! Father tells me that he will take me out the day after tomorrow, that he has already done all the paperwork. . . . But I think I'm better off here, where everything is so familiar. . . .'

Leahu remained silent, uncertain as to what the gentleman expected to hear.

'What do you think, Andrei?' Puiu asked after a while.

'I think you should do whatever you think is best', the guard answered cautiously. 'You know better, as an educated man. . . .'

'I will not move, Andrei!' Puiu insisted anxiously. 'What if, once I got there, I forgot the Ciuleandra again and I had to torment myself trying to remember it? No, no, better to stay here. . . .'

His eyes filled with a peculiar gleam. Agitated, he started pacing around the room again. After a while, he turned once more to the guard:

'Andrei, I won't take no for an answer, you must dance the Ciuleandra for me!'

'Goodness me, sir, I'm an old man now and I don't think my feet could stand it!' the other complained.

'Don't go telling lies, you're as strong as a bear!'

'It's no use, sir, I haven't the strength', replied the guard. 'Us peasants fade quickly, not like you gentlemen. Hard lives, too much work, not enough food.'

'Then I will show you, boy, how to dance the Ciuleandra!' Puiu shouted out contemptuously.

He shuffled and turned on his feet for a few moments, then interrupted himself, dissatisfied:

'It's not working. . . . It's not coming to me. . . . I've lost it again. . . . Come next door into my room, it will work there!'

In his room, Puiu began again, possessed by the dance, ecstatic, transfigured, until he collapsed once again, exhausted. The whole room was still spinning around him and the world seemed on the verge of collapse. He lay there as still as a corpse. . . .

The guard retreated to his room and said a prayer.

XXVIII

The junior doctor rushed in, announcing that the doctor wanted to see him. It was still early in the morning; the visiting hours had not yet started. Wearily, Puiu refused:

'I'm not going. . . . I've had enough.'

The junior doctor looked frightened. How could he refuse the doctor's request? If he was calling him in, it was probably on an important matter. Either way, he didn't dare go back to the doctor and tell him that his patient had ignored his invitation. And so, persuaded more by the intern's terrified expression than by his arguments, Puiu agreed to go with him.

In the corridor, outside the doctor's office, he saw a peasant woman carrying a bundle on her back, wearing a heavy red coat and coarse leather boots as they do in the countryside, and peering at him with a queer expression. Without thinking, he paused for a moment and looked straight into her eyes. He felt that he knew her and that look of hers, in particular, intrigued him. Although she did not dare to say a word, the woman also seemed to recognise him.

At last, agitated, Puiu enquired:

'Where are you from, woman?'

'From Argeş, sir, a village called Vărzari', she answered dolefully.

The answer stung him like the lash of a whip. Suddenly he understood: she must have been Mădălina's mother.

'What is her mother doing here?!' The thought struck him like lightning, but he did not say a word, only hurried to escape into the doctor's office. Without waiting to be asked any questions, he rushed towards the doctor as the man was putting on his white coat, preparing to go on his morning visits:

'Doctor, Doctor, who is that woman in the corridor?' The doctor seemed shocked by his outburst and, to avoid a confrontation, attempted to pacify him. After persuading Puiu to sit down, he began:

'Now, sit down and let's talk. . . . It is precisely because of this woman that I have asked you to come to see me. She's your dead wife's mother.'

'Mădălina's mother!' Puiu exclaimed, jumping to his feet. 'I recognised her. It really is her! I remembered her eyes. . . . But what does she want? Is it me that she's after?'

'Easy, now, easy—' the doctor ordered, almost forcing him back down in his seat.

Puiu blanched; the woman's appearance had shaken him to the core and thrown his mind into chaos, and he bit his lips till they bled in order to control himself long enough to listen. More patiently than ever before, the doctor explained that many others from Vărzari, just like this woman, dropped by to seek his advice whenever they had some trouble in Bucharest. However, as it happened that her dead daughter's husband was right here, in his care, he had thought it wise to arrange a meeting between them, to clarify certain things. So, in effect, if Puiu would be willing, he could introduce him right away to Mădălina's mother so that she could talk to him herself. Puiu had no inclination to talk to this woman, the very thought appalled him, but nevertheless he immediately answered that he would see her at once. The doctor, looking satisfied, opened the door and called out into the corridor:

'Come in, now, dear, come in!'

The woman appeared in the doorway but held back, shy and suspicious:

'Good day to you, sir. . . .'

Puiu's burning eyes grasped at her faded features, searching for traces of Mădălina. The woman held his gaze for a second, then immediately turned to the doctor, who had advanced to the middle of the office to address her:

'Look here, dear, this gentleman was your Mădălina's husband!'

'I thought as much when I saw him outside and he stopped to talk to me, but I couldn't believe it', she said, her voice gaining strength with each word. 'He looks much changed, nothing like the gentleman who came to our village and took away my poor Mădălina. . . .'

'Ah, you have changed too since those days, no doubt about it', Puiu interrupted, overcome by an irresistible instinct to say something.

'Well, sir, no wonder, with all the troubles I've had to bear since then!' the woman answered, glumly shaking her head. 'Oh Lord! And now, on top of everything else, Mădălina's death. Only a mother's heart can guess my sorrow when they told me that my poor girl was dead, and killed by the hand of the very gentleman that took her from my house, proud and beautiful as a white flower. . . .'

She continued to weep, fussing at her wet eyes and lips with the corner of her headscarf. The two men were silent. Puiu threw a furtive glance towards Ursu but quickly lowered his eyes before the man could notice. The uncomfortable silence continued, filled with the insistent, somewhat affected weeping of the woman, who eventually began to whine once again:

'My poor little girl begged me not to give her away and I didn't listen to her, but if I had, my darling child wouldn't be buried in the earth, alone amongst strangers, poor thing. . . .'

Puiu burst out, no longer able to control himself:

'And what do you want now, woman? Quickly, tell me what you want!'

As if this were the very sign she had been waiting for, the woman swiftly wiped away her tears and responded simply, without a trace of emotion in her voice:

'Well, when the word got round our village about Mădălina and her dreadful fate, people advised me to call on you and ask for compensation for my loss, since you killed my girl. . . . So here I am.'

Having abruptly finished her speech, she looked first at Ursu, then at Puiu, cunning and misery blurring together in her gaze. Puiu, stung by her words as if by thorns, looked at her impotently, opened his mouth to say something, changed his mind, and only after another minute's silence attempted to speak diffidently, trying to make sense of it all:

'But your Mădălina was adopted by my aunt, who took her in as her own daughter. Mădălina was no longer yours and you no longer had any claim over her.'

'Adopted, you say, adopted!' the woman boldly persisted. 'But I didn't give her to you so that you could kill her, did I? If I had known she was cursed to die by your hand I wouldn't have given her to you for all the treasures of the earth! No question, it's easy enough for your kind, adopting people's children and then strangling them, quelling their souls. But think of my heart, a mother's heart, did I bear her and raise her so that you could wring her neck like she was a chicken? Strangers don't care, that much is clear to see, but a mother is a mother until her dying day!'

A look of revulsion passed across Doctor Ursu's face and as he turned away to hide it, Puiu, shocked and devastated, looked around the room, searching for something to lean on.

Sensing his weakness, the woman rattled on, alternating between tears and recriminations, until the doctor, bored, interrupted:

'That's enough, woman! The gentleman has greater cares on his mind!'

'He might well have his cares, but what about the damages due to me, the mother?'

At this, Ursu lashed out, indignant:

'You should have remembered you're a mother when you gave Mădălina away, not now when she is dead! Do you understand? It is a low thing to come here to try to profit from her death! That's the end of it, woman!'

The woman, confused, started mumbling:

'But they said . . . they sent me to you. . . .'

'To me? When did you ever listen to me?' Ursu retorted, his cheeks flushed and his voice strained. 'And now you want me to teach you how to swindle gentlemen out of money? I have never swindled anyone, ever, as you know! It is I who was deceived, by others, but I always kept my word!'

Doctor Ursu seemed unrecognisable to Puiu. It was as if a different man, whose tortured soul mirrored his own, was uttering those words.

'As you have come all the way here and wasted your money on the journey,' the doctor continued in an admonishing tone, 'you must go to Mr Faranga, his father, a great, wealthy gentleman, and beg him to give you something for your troubles! You understand? And he, out of the kindness and generosity of his soul, will not send you away with nothing, at least for the sake of Mădălina's memory. But don't start talking about recompense for damages, because you'll get an even worse reception there with that kind of insolence!'

'Yes, yes!' Puiu suddenly rejoined, as if the doctor had plucked the words out of his own heart. 'She must go to my father and she must tell him that I want her to have something, to give her a lot of money, for the sake of Mădălina! Please, doctor, make sure it is done, it would give me great pleasure! She doesn't deserve it, but for the sake of Mădălina's soul, he must give it to her without fail!'

He had not noticed that he was crying, and now the tears from his cheeks slid down, in droplets, slowly, onto his chest. A ceaseless ache burrowed into his brain, like an enervating fly, squirming through its every corner. Yet he sat very still, afraid of more excruciating agonies that were waiting to pounce on him at the first opportunity.

The woman, embarrassed, wiped her mouth with the back of her hand, turned to Puiu, grasped his hand and kissed it, mumbling:

'God bless you, sir, good-bye, may God give you health and peace of mind. . . .'

Standing there motionless, Puiu did not respond to her words. He felt the trace of the woman's lips on his hand like a cold stain.

Ursu guided her out the door, his hand pressed into the small of her back:

'That's right, dear. . . . I'll see to it that someone back home lends you a hand if you need any help. . . . But don't go round begging from gentlemen, because it's not worthy of you, dear!'

He escorted her into the corridor.

XXIX

On his return, the doctor found Puiu in the same position, his moist eyes fixed on a point on the wall. Following his gaze, the doctor noticed that he was looking at a photograph above his desk. Gently, seeming afraid of disturbing his thoughts, he muttered:

'These people! There was nothing else I could do, I had to intervene, it was appalling!'

The voice seemed to drift over Puiu from another world, while his vagabond thoughts wandered elsewhere, raking through details benumbed by forgetfulness, struggling to piece out of them a semblance of a life or at least some coherent memories. He realised that he ought to answer but no words came to mind. Then, suddenly, he shuddered, trying to quench a reservoir of tears. He squeezed his eyes shut and the last teardrops stumbled down his cheeks, cleansing the orbs that shone with a new living light, his gaze burning with the fitful glimmer of a flame on the verge of being extinguished. His thoughts now arranged themselves obediently, clear and gleaming like brightly coloured beads on a delicate thread, and his voice rang out, shaking off its irritating hoarseness:

'Thank you, Doctor! I thought you were a cruel man, but now I am touched by your kindness.'

Doctor Ursu smiled, waving away the remark.

'No, it's true! You were good even to Mădălina's mother!' Puiu insisted, then softly added: 'How well you seem to know each other! You knew Mădălina too, didn't you, Doctor?'

'Yes, . . .' Ursu murmured, darkening.

'You must have known her well, before my time, a long time before?' Puiu insisted.

'We were neighbours, so naturally I knew her when she was a child', the doctor assented, in a smothered voice. 'But I was much older than her, a good ten years. . . .'

Puiu's veins seemed to fill with fire. A tide of questions swarmed through his mind, yet he couldn't set them loose all at once lest the doctor would shrink away into his old self, like a miserly inquisitor. He allowed a few more moments to pass before probing him again:

'Then surely you must know about the time we were at Vărzari, at the Ciuleandra, Doctor?'

'I was a student, on holiday', Ursu answered.

'Now I know everything, Doctor, everything!' Puiu cried, losing control as he rushed towards the photograph hanging above the desk. 'You were there when I danced the Ciuleandra and when I kissed Mădălina! You were there and Mădălina looked straight at you, I remember it now. You were standing by a tree, a few steps away, and you were watching me the whole time, only me, and you saw me kissing her. I was on fire, nothing else mattered except for the Ciuleandra and Mădălina and I saw you only as in a dream, but now I see you clearly, as if I were standing beside you. Look, you had exactly the same expression as you do in that photograph, that's why it's haunted me since the first time I saw it. It is true, isn't it, Doctor? Tell me! Tell me!'

'It's true', the doctor consented simply.

Puiu collapsed into the office chair, vanquished by the raw light all around him. The emotion choked him. He had so many questions prepared, yet they all now imploded to dust. A single one darted straight out of his heart:

'Doctor, did you love Mădălina?' and Doctor Ursu, as if he had been waiting for this very question, his hands behind his back, slowly swaying from side to side, looked him in the eye and said without a flicker of bashfulness:

'I loved her a great deal, yes. . . . She was only a young girl, but I loved her like a sister, and a wife. . . . In those days I was sentimental and had bourgeois aspirations. The pinnacle of happiness seemed to me to have my own practice in my own county, to marry Mădălina, to make her into a lady, to love her and for her to love me, to have children and live until the age of seventy. I told her all this and she understood me, even though she seemed in other ways a mere child. We had her mother's blessing, that woman who called on me just now to help her blackmail you into making a profit out of Mădălina's death.

Although I was poor, I did as much as I could to help her, my future mother-in-law, this woman. Everything was going well. I had two more years of study before I would start making my own living. And then you turned up as we danced the Ciuleandra. Straight away, I had a dreadful feeling when I saw you sitting on the verandah of that inn. And then, when you joined in the dance and clung onto Mădălina, I understood what that feeling meant. I tried to fight it, to prevent what was fated to happen. When they called her to meet the gentlemen, I didn't want to let her go. They took her away from me anyway. You left and I felt I could breathe again. I thought we had escaped. Yet the next day I spoke at length to Mădălina, I clenched her hand, her hot, rough hand, and looked into her eyes: 'Don't go, Mădălina! Don't leave me on my own!' And with all her heart she answered: 'I won't go!' And then, when I was away from home you came and you took her.

Never in my life have I cried, so I didn't cry then. But I took my anger out on the innkeeper and left him bleeding. I had heard that he had been the negotiator in the whole business and earned himself a healthy tip from you gentlemen. And that is how all my happy dreams of bourgeois matrimony went up in a puff of smoke. There was no reason for me to hanker after the post of a provincial doctor, so I came here. Yet I could not blot out the memory of Mădălina from my heart. I heard about her good fortune, her successes in high society, and never once did I try to get near her. To be honest, I lived with the illusion that deep in her heart she loved only me, and I confess I was afraid that this fantasy might turn to dust. Against my will, fate brought me one day face to face with Mrs Faranga.

I was introduced to her like any other stranger. She was startled for a second, then shook my hand and we exchanged the conventional pleasantries. That was all. Still I was satisfied because in her eyes—I can now tell you this—I saw that she hadn't forgotten me and I understood that she would have given up all her riches and splendour for that modest rural life we had dreamt of together long ago. I only caught a few glimpses of her after that, she in an elegant limousine, me in some rickety hansom, travelling in different directions towards our separate worlds. I greeted her courteously and she responded simply.

We were casual acquaintances. Perhaps in the depths of my heart I still nursed the hope that Mădălina would miraculously be returned to me, and perhaps she dreamed the same dreams. One morning, however, a month and two days ago, as I was finishing my shift, the doctor on duty informed me that the previous night the son of the former minister Faranga had been admitted to our hospital after suffering a nervous breakdown and strangling his wife. I can't vouch for what expression my face arranged itself in at that moment, but my soul squirmed like a worm quashed underfoot. It was the irrefutable end of any hope of a miracle!'

Ursu had given up any attempt to contain himself. His perpetual smile gave his trembling voice a hard, ironic edge. Puiu was roused by every word he uttered, his body doused in sweat. His eyes were glued to his lips, he drank in every modulation of his voice, as if witnessing a revelation. He burst out, in ecstasy:

'Yet I loved her more, doctor! I loved her so much that I killed her!'

The doctor glared at him, his pity mingled with hatred:

'You are right. . . . You killed her twice, even; you snuffed out her soul when you took her away, and then you slayed her body! You are right!'

Puiu, wide-eyed, cried out:

'Now I know why I strangled her, doctor! I now know the reason why! It was because of you!'

'Even though you didn't know I existed?' Ursu mocked.

'I didn't know it, but I could feel it all the same!' Puiu declared triumphantly. 'When I looked into her eyes, I couldn't see myself there, but somebody else! Those beautiful eyes never once smiled back at me! Her melancholy closeted her away from me, mourning for the one she had lost. Her soul locked me out, no matter how hard she tried to pretend. And then, when I understood that she would forever be a stranger, when I understood that there was no hope that I could ever win her heart, I destroyed her, so she could never belong to another! So you see how I discovered on my own the reason that you have toiled for so many weeks to pluck out of me? The patient is the best doctor when it comes to understanding the malady of the soul!'

Gradually, Doctor Ursu regained his composure. When he spoke, his voice took on a cold, professional tone:

'So, Mr Faranga. The hand of fate has improbably brought you into my care, in your hour of need. As we are about to part ways, I can tell you that in my opinion you killed your wife without any premeditation, by accident. Clearly, without your knowledge, destiny has used you as an instrument to destroy me. For a moment, and only a moment, I was tempted to make you suffer in the way that I've suffered. But the physician in me overpowered the wounded man. Now that the doctor's duty has come to an end, you have heard the voice of that man. I have made my diagnosis and will deliver it to the committee. You are blameless in this matter, just as you were innocent of any wrong when you took away Mădălina from Vărzari!'

Puiu could not follow the doctor's argument, yet, for the sake of his dignity, felt indebted to answer him:

'We were rivals, yet we didn't even know one another!'

Doctor Ursu interrupted him brusquely:

'We were doctor and patient. That's all that matters. The rest is mere fog. You suffered, it passed, and all that is left is a patient standing in front of his doctor and a doctor facing his conscience.'

Unsteadily, Puiu left the office, feeling that his knees were about to give way. He walked down the corridor slowly, his arms hanging like dead weights by his sides, as if they didn't belong to him. Doctor Ursu escorted him out and watched him until he vanished from sight.

XXX

All day, Puiu Faranga sat glumly by the window looking out into the garden, listening to the irritating drumming of a rain so fine it seemed to have been sifted out of the clouds. The rain, the garden, the whole world meant nothing to him. Shadows danced before his eyes, strange, elusive ghosts that he couldn't swat away, yet they no longer mattered either. Occasionally a thought would surface out of the depths of his mind; he would follow it for a while, like a wisp of smoke, then, bored, let it drift away. . . .

When the sky began to darken, he remembered something, stood up, opened the door, and looked into the antechamber. The guard was reading a newspaper, whispering each word with great care so as not to disturb the gentleman. Instinctively, he took a step towards him, then stopped as if he had taken the wrong path. He turned back to the window, and as the darkness was closing in, he felt his feet possessed by an irresistible desire to skip into a dance. He smiled contentedly and began to hum. The tune came to him immediately. And then the dance began to take shape. . . .

By the end of the evening he was so exhausted that the guard had to help him undress and put him to bed like a child. His face was aglow with ecstasy, and sweat streamed down his gaunt cheeks.

The following day he woke up tired, yet as soon as he climbed out of bed his body felt as light as a snowflake.

He began to dance again, from time to time asking the guard questions while the man, busy getting the room in order for the doctor's visit, tried his best to answer them. But Puiu was not really interested in his answers anyway, his questions merely a pretence at normal conversation while his brain whirled away frenetically, trying to hatch the plan that would lead him to his great redemption.

At last they could hear, through the open doors, the doctor's footsteps echoing in the corridor.

He was seized with panic that his plan would not succeed. The pounding of his heart made him sick; he crossed his arms over his chest to still it. Then the doctor entered, morose and severe as usual, sniffing out anything amiss in the room. The guard stood alert by the door of the antechamber. Behind the doctor, Puiu spotted a new nurse, an old woman with glasses balanced on the tip of her nose, carrying some official documents.

'So, what's new. . . ? Feeling better?' the doctor asked, as usual.

'Very well, doctor, excellent!' Puiu enthused, and, after a brief pause, added triumphantly: 'I'm particularly joyful because I have danced the Ciuleandra for two hours and still I am not tired!'

The junior doctor stifled a hoot of laughter, but Ursu encouraged him, fascinated:

'Really. . . ? Then all your troubles are over?'

'Oh no, one thing still troubles me greatly!' Puiu quickly answered. 'And I must speak to you about it right away.'

'Do you want to tell me now or do you wish to speak to me privately?' the doctor asked, concerned.

'Privately?' Puiu spat out. 'Real redemption cannot spring from private confessions, Doctor! It can only be granted when everything is out in the open, for everyone to hear!'

His voice softened and continued sorrowfully:

'When we first met, Doctor—and everyone knows why I'm here—I had some very low intentions. I can confess them now openly and without any embarrassment, particularly as they were my father's idea and I just accepted them without thinking. I came to you, Doctor, having done you-know-what, to pretend that I was mad and in that way escape from justice. You took me in good faith, I give you credit for that, you conducted some tests and asked me questions. . . . But now, because this sickening farce must come to an end, I have to confess everything, because I can no longer bear the lies, Doctor! This is why I want to declare in front of everyone here present that I'm not mad and that I want to pay for my crime!'

Doctor Ursu thought for a few moments, then murmured:

'Yes, yes. . . .' The hesitation in his voice goaded Puiu. He felt that he needed to reinforce his point more vehemently:

'There is no doubt about it, Doctor! Please make a note immediately, stating that I'm not mad!'

'Of course, of course, but . . .' the doctor began to soothe him.

Then Puiu took a step back and with fiery eyes whispered:

'You mean, you think I *am* mad. . . . You mean . . .'

Like a beast, he threw himself on the doctor, his hands clenched around his neck, shouting:

'Quiet! Quiet! Quiet!'

The junior doctor and the guard rushed to Ursu's aid, even though the doctor had already grabbed hold of his patient's arms and immobilised him. The nurse ran out of the room, horrified. The guard held Puiu in his arms as he continued moaning:

'Quiet! Quiet!'

Regaining his composure, Doctor Ursu retreated to the antechamber and gave the order:

'Let him go now and lock the door!'

They threw Puiu onto the bed but he sprang back and threw himself against the door, screaming:

'I am not mad! I am not mad! I am not mad!'

Yet after a few minutes he calmed down, as if suddenly awake, then stumbled towards the window, looking towards the garden, quietly whistling. He could feel his calf muscles twitching and murmured contentedly:

'Ciuleandra . . .'

Doctor Ursu was watching him from the other side of the door, through the observation window. Seeing him begin to dance again, he moved away with a frown and ordered the junior doctor:

'Call Mr Faranga immediately and ask him to come to see me at the hospital today, without fail. Let's say, around four?'

'Certainly', the other replied, jotting down the time in his notebook.

XXXI

At four o'clock precisely, old Faranga entered the doctor's office. He rushed into the room, his breathing a little laboured, and collapsed immediately into the chair the doctor offered him, vaguely apologising.

'I have asked you to come here, Your Excellency—'

Faranga, forgetting his exhaustion, cut in eagerly:

'I was planning to come here today anyway, dear sir, even before I received your invitation. I have some news to tell you regarding my boy. At last, now that there is nothing left to fear, I feel I can confess to you that ever since my son's arrival here has given you the opportunity to be of service to our family and to show us some goodwill, I have been struck by your disquieting reticence. This is why I felt that I had to intervene and have arranged that Puiu should be moved to another sanatorium, where I hope I will be shown more consideration and sympathy. The move was scheduled for today but my son, under the spell of a hysterical superstition undoubtedly brought on by the stress he has suffered, developed an aversion to the date, the thirteenth of March, so he is due to leave here tomorrow. As you can see, it was my duty to inform you of the hospital board's decision. Therefore, with the wisdom granted to me by my age and experience, I would like to leave you today with some advice: a doctor should never forget that, above all, he is still a human being!'

'I never forgot that, Your Excellency, I was decidedly

human from the beginning to the end', the doctor responded, with the flicker of an ironic smile.

'To be honest, I hadn't noticed', Faranga replied in the same tone.

'In that case, I can only apologise', the doctor summed up, with deliberate emphasis. 'But with respect to this move to another sanatorium, I'm afraid you have wasted your time. . . .'

'What? How do you mean?' The old man startled, terrified that this savage had made it his mission to destroy his son with a damaging report.

'What I mean, Your Excellency, is that your son is seriously ill and must be committed to an asylum!' said Doctor Ursu, his grave tone giving Faranga no room to protest.

Bewildered, the old man struggled to understand, unsure whether he should be alarmed or glad that the doctor finally believed their story. He stared at the doctor helplessly until the man, sensing his confusion, added:

'Two weeks ago, I thought I had reached a verdict regarding your son's case, Your Excellency. I had even written my report—look, it's there, on my desk—in which I stated that I believed your son to have diminished responsibility for the murder of his wife, as the crime had clearly taken place during a nervous breakdown. I merely continued my observations in order to decide whether I should recommend that he should spend a few months in a special sanatorium, to recuperate, or whether he was ready to go back to his normal life. Yesterday I would have suggested the latter. . . . He seemed tranquil, rational, normal. But today's events have shattered all these assumptions and turned that report on my desk into a useless piece of paper. . . .'

Pale and broken, the old man stood up, with a hoarse whisper:

'Doctor, can I see him?'

'I will take you to him, Your Excellency', said Ursu, allowing the trembling old man to lean on him for support.

In the antechamber, the guard clicked his heels and gave a military salute.

'How's the patient?' Ursu asked him, nodding towards Puiu's room.

'With respect, still dancing, Sir!' Ursu opened the observation window in the door and beckoned Faranga to look inside. Bare-chested, his pyjama shirt unbuttoned, Puiu hopped on the spot, humming a broken melody with intense concentration, his face pouring with sweat and glowing with ecstasy. After watching him for a few moments, the old man, unable to contain himself any longer, called out his name. Still dancing, Puiu turned his head and beamed at his father:

'*C'est Ciuleandra, vous savez. . . ?* It's Ciuleandra, Papa, you know. *Vous m'avez permis, n'est ce pas?* You said I could! It was you who told me, "Go ahead!" So you can't be angry, Papa! *Et puis c'est très amusant . . . ou. . . . très . . .* It's so much fun. . . . yes. . . . very . . .'

Old Faranga sank down onto the edge of the guard's bed. His despair took his breath away. Only his eyes, as though with a life of their own, welled up and spilled their tears, soaking that majestic, impeccably groomed beard. He could hear Doctor Ursu by his side, attempting to console him with complex, meaningless medical terms. At last the old man asked him:

'Is there any hope, Doctor? Any hope at all?'

Ursu shrugged:

'Only God can perform miracles!'

In the next room they could hear Puiu's feet pounding on the floorboards, their frenetic rhythm urged on by the choked murmur of a melody, as hoarse as a dying man's last breath.

Contributors

Gabi Reigh was born in Romania and moved to the UK in her teens. She has won the Stephen Spender prize for poetry in translation and is currently engaged in a translation project called 'Interbellum Series' focusing on works from the Romanian interwar period. The first titles in this series were *Poems of Light* by Lucian Blaga and three works by Mihail Sebastian: *The Town with Acacia Trees*, *Women* and *The Star with No Name*.

George T. Sipos is Associate Professor at the West University of Timisoara, in Romania, where he teaches Japanese literature, language and culture. His research focuses on modern and contemporary Japanese society and literature from a transcultural perspective, in particular on comparative research on Japan and Romania's modernity, modern nation state, activism, and resistance against state oppression. He published extensively on modern and contemporary Romanian literature, as well as four volumes of Japanese literature in Romanian translation. His most recent publications include 'Journeys of Political Self-Discovery: The Writings of Miyamoto Yuriko and Panait Istrati from late 1920s Soviet Russia' (*Human and Social Studies*, 2018), and book chapters on the works of Mishima Yukio (in *Mishima Monogatari: Un samurai delle arti*, 2020), Kawabata Yasunari and Akutagawa Ryūnosuke (in *Critical Insights: Modern Japanese Literature*, 2017). A co-edited volume on Japan's interwar society and literature is coming out from Routledge, and he is currently preparing a single-authored study on Japan's *tenkō* and *tenkō* literature phenomenon of the 1930s, due to be published in 2021.

Daniele Serra is an Italian illustrator and comic book artist. His main influences and inspirations arrive from weird and horror fiction written by H. P. Lovecraft and William H. Hodgson, Ridley Scott movies, Japanese horror films and Clive Barker's works.

His love for horror culture started before his painting career, making him quickly develop his signature style: high contrast paintings with bright, as well as strong dark colors, curved strokes and shadows, and a particular attention to his character's gaze and expression.

He has handled a diverse and growing range of work including Clive Barker's *Hellraiser*, *The Crow: Memento Mori*, Joe R. Lansdale's "I Tell you it's Love," *Tommyknockers* by Stephen King, *Voices from the Borderland* by William Hope Hodgson, *Hellraiser: The Toll* by Alan Miller, *Deep Like the River* by Tim Waggoner, and *Frankenstein in London* by Brian Stableford, among others.

He can be reached at https://www.danieleserra.com/

Lightning Source UK Ltd.
Milton Keynes UK
UKHW010729271222
414464UK00001B/188